Totally Bound P

Knigh
\

MW01051597

WHAT YOU SEE

FAITH ASHLIN

What You See
ISBN # 978-1-78430-153-8
©Copyright Faith Ashlin 2014
Cover Art by Posh Gosh ©Copyright July 2014
Interior text design by Claire Siemaszkiewicz
Totally Bound Publishing

Published in 2014 by Totally Bound Publishing, Newland House, The Point, Weaver Road, Lincoln, LN6 3QN, United Kingdom.

Totally Bound Publishing is an imprint of Total-E-Ntwined Limited.

WHAT YOU SEE

Dedication

For Alison, I wouldn't have started without you

Chapter One

Last chance, Richard thought, hand on the dirty, flaking door. Last chance to change his mind and walk away. What he was doing went against everything he and Grady had been working for, fighting for. He needed to walk away right now.

Only then he'd be back up shit creek with no sensible alternative, no way of making this better, no way of keeping it secret. At least if he did it like this he would be giving someone a chance, setting him up for a decent life. Yeah, that was how he should think of it. That didn't make it right, though, and Grady would have shot him down in flames in a second.

"Fucking, fucking... Fuck," he finished lamely, hand still in place. He took a deep breath, exhaling slowly and carefully. He'd give whoever it was a choice— make him an offer, like they said in the movies. If he said no then fair enough, Richard would walk away. No harm done. At least the kid would be a bit better off and that had to be a good thing.

He looked around him. It was the sleaziest part of town, full of drunks and addicts, crime and hookers.

Dirty and broken. He'd be doing a good deed for everyone if he torched the place and watched it burn. If this was where the guy had ended up, with the kind of people who were inside, then he was doing him a real favor. He rolled his shoulders, set his face in a hard scowl, and tapped lightly on the door.

It was opened almost immediately by two men nearly as slimy and filthy as the building. They nodded at him, backing away almost deferentially, and waited for him to pass inside. He was hit first by the smell. It was rank and sour, the stench of old piss and even older misery.

Paxman was sitting opposite the door in a faded green armchair with half its stuffing missing. It seemed the likely source of the smell. Paxman grinned, his rotten teeth showing, trying to act bigger and more dangerous than he was. He was a midlevel opportunist crook, all too familiar in the chaos of the changing world order. Richard hated him on sight. But he was useful. Grady had taught him to remember that, until there was the time and resources to do something about people like him, it was a good idea to keep them where you could use them.

"Richard, good to see you, man, have a drink." Paxman pointed at a bottle of cheap whiskey. "Take the weight off your feet."

Richard shook his head, trying to hide his disgust. "No thanks. I believe you have something for me."

"What's the rush?" Paxman tried, but Richard's face was set in hard lines. "Okay, okay, I'll get my boys to bring it out." With that he waved his hand and the two men who'd opened the door pushed off the wall and headed into another room, deeper in the building. "I think you're going to like it." He winked, nasty and crude. "Not a patch on Grady, of course, but I reckon this one's ripe for using."

Richard fought down the urge to wipe the grin from Paxman's face with his fist. What the fuck gave scum like that the right to say Grady's name or to imply Richard would use anyone? He could do it, easy as shit, could almost see his fist in the guy's face. But if he did that he'd end up walking away without what he came for. He pressed his lips tightly together.

There was a brief sound of a scuffle, then the inner door opened again and the two men came back pushing a tall, scruffy young man. Richard couldn't see his face. His head was down and his long dirty hair fell over it, but there were bruises on his wrists where the metal cuffs bit into them and his bones were starting to protrude. This one hadn't eaten enough for a long time and if Richard had thought the building was filthy, it had nothing on the kid. His clothes were thin and useless in the current cold weather, only held together by dirt—and he stank.

Richard longed to reach out a helping hand, the same way he'd done so many times before that it had become an automatic response. But now wasn't the time or place to show weakness.

Paxman was talking, shooting off about the kid faster than a flowing rapid. Richard only caught the tail end of it. "Told you on the phone he was a fine figure. Now you can see what I'm talking about. Tall as all fuck and muscles on him too. Good enough for anything you want." The leer was back, nasty and rough.

Richard stared him down but didn't say a word. "You'll be wanting to see what you're paying for, though, only fucking fair." Paxman kicked out, his heavy boot connecting with the kid's ankle. "Boy, get your clothes off. Let the man have a good look at what you're packing."

Again Richard wanted to intervene, to say no. But right now he had a part to play, and if they were all going to get out of this safely, he had to play it right.

The young man raised his head, his long, thin face empty, and stared into nothing. He held his cuffed hands in front of him and waited, without moving, as the restraints were removed.

"You try anything and you'll be dead before you reach the fucking door," Paxman said as he unlocked them.

The kid looked like he hadn't heard, slipping his thin jacket and his shirt off as though it were the most ordinary thing in the world. Richard knew it probably was. He pressed his lips even more tightly together and folded his arms across his chest.

Quickly, efficiently, the guy stripped all his clothes off, his boxers sliding too easily from his narrow hips. The pile on the floor looked more like rags than clothes. Then he stood, without a trace of embarrassment, tall and almost proud, his arms hanging at his sides, staring into nothing, his eyes perfectly blank.

It was as Richard had expected, dirt ground in so deep it'd take a month of scrubbing to get it off. Bruises, cuts and grazes, some old, some newer, bones sticking out where there should have been flesh. This one had been on the street too long, but underneath there was muscle and strength. He'd do as well as anyone.

If he agreed.

"You want a closer look?" Paxman asked. "Hell, have a free fuck for all I care. I made sure he was clean, took him down to that clinic on Park Street myself. Got a certificate and everything. Go on, have a feel."

"No," Richard said flatly. "I'll take him."

"Course you will." Paxman smirked. "You can't wait to get him somewhere quiet and bend him over a—"

"You need to shut your mouth right now," Richard said, and Paxman had the sense to do as he was told. Richard pulled out a roll of money from an inside pocket then held it out toward him. "Take it and get out of here."

"Hey, hey, hey." Paxman held his hands up. "We need to negotiate here. I quoted a price before I saw how fine the merchandise was."

"Take it and get out," Richard repeated, his voice quiet and hard

Paxman licked nervously at his lips, rubbing his palms on the fabric covering his thighs. His gaze flickered over the kid one more time, then at Richard. Richard could guess what he was thinking. The guy might be worth more but Paxman knew better than to argue.

He grabbed the roll from Richard's outstretched hand as he went past. "Good doing business with you. Only next time I won't give a price up front. I mean, I..." With one last glance at Richard he scuttled out, pushing his men out of the way in his haste.

The door slammed hard then it was just Richard and the kid in the room. The very naked kid.

"Get dressed and let's get out of here before more of his kind show up," Richard said, walking over to stare through the grimy window. All he wanted now was to be as far away from here as possible. Behind him he could hear the sound of clothes being put back on and he deliberately didn't turn round until it was quiet again.

When he did move the kid was fully clothed, looking down at the handcuffs and key still on the floor. Richard followed his gaze then glanced back up. Dark, intense eyes met his for the first time. Eyes that a person could spend a lifetime trying to understand.

"You could run now," Richard said gently. "I could probably stop you, but I won't. How about I buy you all you can eat and we talk? At the end of that, if you want to go, I won't stop you, but at least you'll have a full belly. What do you say?"

The young man stared at him for a long, long moment then nodded once, a short quick movement.

Richard nodded with him and headed for the door but stopped and turned, hesitating for a second before saying, "I'm Richard. And you are...?"

Again the kid simply stood still, watching Richard. It was just as Richard was starting to feel like a fool that he spoke. "Denny. My name's Denny."

Without thinking, Richard stuck his hand out. There was an awkward moment while Denny looked at it, before his gaze flicked up to Richard's face and he reached out to shake his hand. His grip was strong and powerful and more confident than Richard had expected. For some reason that gave him a little hope.

* * * *

He took Denny to a small Italian restaurant on the other side of town. He was known there. The owners were friendly to the cause and wouldn't ask questions. The two of them would be left alone in a secluded corner to talk. Richard watched as Denny ate his way through half the menu while he just picked at a plate of pasta. Sensibly, Richard also stuck to coffee, although he was sorely tempted to order whiskey. But he knew he needed a clear head for the goddamned awful conversation that was going to come.

Richard drew it out as long as possible, offering cake, ice cream, coffee and anything else he could think of. In the end it was just him and Denny, two half-empty cups between them and a mouth so dry Richard wasn't sure he could speak even if he wanted to.

Even if he knew what to say.

He smoothed a hand over the red-checked tablecloth and felt the weight of Denny's eyes and expectation on him. Now. He needed to speak now. He felt as inarticulate as a newborn as the silence stretched on.

It was Denny who spoke first, ignoring the pressure of that silence. "You said you wanted to talk. If you've changed your mind, I'll go now." But he didn't move.

"No, I…" Richard plucked at his napkin. "Don't go yet, I… My name's Richard."

"You already told me that," Denny said when the quiet threatened to become too long again. "Anything else you want to say?"

"A deal," Richard dropped in quickly before he had a chance to change his mind. "I want to offer you a deal."

"What kind of deal?" Denny asked, pushing his hair out of his eyes.

"I…" Again Richard couldn't help the hesitation. "Let's talk about you for a minute first. How old are you?"

"Twenty-five."

So, not a kid then. "Tell me about yourself."

"Nothing much to say." Denny shook his head, laying his palms flat on the table. "You know who I am, what I am."

"You were a slave, right? Before the uprising?" Richard asked softly.

"I was even after." Denny leaned back, hands staying out in front of him. "I was at a place right up the mountains. Things moved real slow there, freedom even slower. I saw on TV that it was supposed to have changed but I was still kept under lock and key and no one came to stop them."

"I'm sorry. That's not how it should have been."

"Not your fault." Denny hitched a shoulder almost nonchalantly.

"Yeah, in a way it kind of is. But you weren't the only one and I wouldn't bet on the fact that there aren't others still being held." Denny stayed silent and still at that. "How did you get away?"

"They got careless when I was out working. I started walking and just kept right on going." He shrugged again. It was a simple straightforward movement but Richard could see what lay behind it. "I thought it'd be easy. I couldn't have been more wrong."

"What happened?" It sounded like this kid hadn't really talked in a long time, had almost forgotten how. Maybe now was the time to start. "What happened between then and now? It must be a couple of years."

"Took me long enough to get down from the mountains. I had to keep hiding out and I knew there was no one in those parts that would help me. Of course it was winter and I thought I'd either starve or freeze to death. But I didn't, I made it down. Things weren't a lot better when I did."

"But there are supposed to be places in the towns to help, people who can get you food, a place to stay." Richard knew about these. Hell, he'd helped organize them.

Again the laconic shrug from Denny. "I was about a year too late. They were more interested in education programs and training than in people like me. I had enough trouble getting my papers, seeing as how I still had my slave brands." He pulled up his sleeve and rolled his hand over, showing the ownership markings on the inside of his wrist. "Turns out I hadn't been properly registered anyway. No one knew I was there so apparently that made it harder to make me free."

"But they did? You got your freedom papers?"

Denny gave a curt nod. "Didn't do me a lot of good. Three nights later I was sleeping rough again and they were stolen. Then I got picked up by the law for vagrancy and told to clear out of town. I couldn't get any work, so no money." Another shrug, one full of more emotion than all the others—but only if you looked hard enough for it. "I ended up right back on the streets. When your friend Paxman caught me it was almost a relief. At least as a slave, even a black market one, you usually get fed."

"Paxman's no friend of mine," Richard insisted.

"You're the one that bought me from him." Denny leveled his eyes on Richard.

"I don't own you. You're free now. It's not the first time I've paid for someone's freedom and I don't suppose it'll be the last. I could have got you the official way but..." He shook his head.

"If you're just going to let me go, why'd you bother?" Denny asked.

"Later." Richard held up a hand as if to stop the question from reaching him. "First tell me what kind of slave you were."

Denny pursed his lips. "The worker kind, like most." When Richard sat still, waiting for more, he went on.

"I did all the repairs, built fences, dealt with the animals, did a bit of heavy work on the land. Normal stuff."

"And..." Richard slicked his tongue over his lip, fighting to keep his attention on Denny's face. "Were you a pleasure slave?"

A casual shrug this time. "Some. You weren't allowed to say no, remember?"

"I know." Richard nodded. "You get hurt bad?"

"Didn't really get hurt at all, especially not during sex." Denny scratched at his cheek before curling his hand around his cup. "They were mostly old, didn't want anything fancy. The only times I really got hurt were when I tried to run, when I was younger. Beat me good and proper then, they would."

Richard took a breath then exhaled the question, "When it comes to sex, what do you like, men or women?"

"Both." Denny watched him levelly.

"I know you didn't have an option but do you have a preference?"

"If I have a choice? Guys."

"You any good at it? I mean, do you know what you're doing?"

"In bed?" Denny tilted his head, gaze even stronger on Richard's face. "Yeah, I know how to make sure everyone has a good time. You learn how to. Gets it over with quicker and leaves everyone happier. Why?"

This was it, the golden question, the moment of truth. Richard's belly turned over on a wave of adrenaline or fear like he hadn't felt for a long, long time. But he'd already made the decision. Now it was time to follow through. He sat up straighter and looked at Denny as steadily as he could. "Because I'm offering you a deal, a job if you like."

"What deal?"

"I'll get you your papers, but that's not part of it. You get them even if you say no because they're yours by right. I'll have your brands removed. You'll be left with a scar but there's no way around that. You stay with me for a while, you get all the food you want, some decent clothes, and I'll pay you. Money in your hand or the bank, however you like it. After, I'll set you up with whatever suits you—a job, training, introductions, somewhere to live." Richard couldn't seem to stop talking, even though he knew he was only trying to delay the inevitable.

Denny seemed to be considering it, his finger running over the cup handle. "What do I have to do for all that?"

Richard inhaled very carefully. "You have to teach me. Teach me what to do in bed."

Denny's eyes widened but he didn't react otherwise. "You want me to be a whore or a sex therapist?"

"I was thinking more along the sex therapist lines but that's probably just me being naïve or optimistic," Richard admitted.

"You a virgin?"

"No." Richard shook his head. "I just don't... I don't have much experience. Hardly any, really."

"You're kidding, right? I mean, you're fucking gorgeous. You could get anyone you want without even asking."

"Never wanted anybody but one guy," Richard said quietly.

"And he didn't want you?"

"Yeah, he did. It just wasn't as simple as that."

"Why not?" Denny asked straight out.

Fuck it, Richard figured Denny was going to find out sooner or later. He might as well get it over and done with now.

"You ever heard of Grady Porter?"

"Of course I have." Denny sat up, the name suddenly animating him. "It was his death that spurred on the whole uprising, that got everyone released. If he hadn't died when he did, then thousands of slaves would still be... Jesus fucking shit, are you Grady Porter's Richard? The guy that was always with him? His...his..."

"Partner? Lover? Whatever you want to call it. Yeah, I'm Grady's Richard."

"Fucking hell." Denny rocked with astonishment as his mouth widened to match his eyes. "Grady Porter's Richard, right here, right in front of me. Man, you must have been through some serious shit. You were out fighting while I was cleaning out horse crap."

"We were." Richard gaze fell to the scar on the back of his hand and he remembered, just for a moment. "But the war's supposed to be over. We've been fighting for peace for the last three years, trying to clear up the mess. You should have been out a long time ago."

"I guess you couldn't do everything at once." Denny was still shaking his head and staring, looking stunned.

"Funny, but Grady wouldn't have agreed with you on that one." Richard smiled a tight little smile.

"But he's been dead, what, over four years?"

"Five next March."

"I don't get it. So?"

"He was the only person I've ever wanted, the only one I've ever slept with." Again Richard's voice was soft and low.

"But if you were with him? Fuck man, I saw you on TV once. Watched when I shouldn't have just so I could hear what he sounded like, see him move. It was so much better than a picture in a ripped-up newspaper. I don't think I really looked at you but I remember the way he was hanging on to your hand, the way he looked at you. He loved you."

"I know," Richard said, and the smile was back, easier this time. "And I loved him. But it wasn't as simple as that."

"Why?"

It felt like Denny wasn't about to let him get away with anything.

Richard collapsed back into the chair and ran a hand slowly over his closed eyes. So many memories, so long ago. When he opened them again Denny was watching him, waiting with a stillness Richard knew he'd had to learn over the years.

"I fell in love with Grady when I was sixteen and he was a couple of years older. He was my father's pleasure slave, although pleasure certainly wasn't the word he would've used. I used to listen to his screams at night, then patch him up when my father and his friends were finished with him. I loved him, he loved me, but what could anyone do in that world? They'd have killed him if they found out. Made me watch as they did it before whipping me to the bone. I don't know, maybe we would have gone on like that. But one night, after, when I went to him, I couldn't bring him around, couldn't stop his bleeding."

He stopped talking, staring across the table at memories that were years old but as clear as day. "My father came in, saw us, and made a grab for Grady. I couldn't let that… I hit him, hard as I could with a baseball bat. I thought I killed him. So I bundled up

Grady, took any money and stuff I could find, and drove off. There I was, eighteen, on the run, and with no idea where to go. It took me about six months of stealing and hiding and trying to nurse Grady back to health before we found others like us. Others who wanted to fight the system. That's how the freedom movement started, a bunch of us runaways plus a few intellectuals who were anti-slavery. I've spent the rest of my life fighting for it. Even after Grady died, I carried on because what else was I going to do? That's what he would have wanted."

His gaze went back to Denny's eyes, holding them fast. "I'm not complaining. We did good and we had a lot of years together, but... After what had been done to him, sex wasn't high up on Grady's list of things to do. We kissed and hugged and slept clinging tightly to each other for years but... We tried things at first, only Grady didn't enjoy... I didn't blame him, how could I? For most of the time we were together my sex life consisted of him jerking me off and he didn't even want me to return the favor. Since he died?" He shrugged, deep and ironic. "I've just exchanged his hand for mine."

"So what's changed? Why do you want to do it now?"

"Because I guess it's time to move on. Some of the others in the movement want to build alliances, think toward the future. There's a guy who's interested in me, Gino Simms. He's okay, nice enough. I could do a lot worse. A link with him would make the movement even more secure, give it financial stability and strength. So why not? If not him then someone like him, it doesn't really matter who. The actual guy isn't important." He stopped, taking a deep breath then letting it out slowly. "Only, I don't want to get into anything knowing nothing. I don't want to be vulnerable. People look at me and think I'm one thing, but I'm not. I want to be in control, to be prepared. So I need someone to teach me."

"You're going to sleep with some guy just to build an alliance?" Denny said incredulously.

"You've been made to do worse. Hell, I'm still asking you to do it for money. What's the difference?"

"I had no choice." Denny's voice rose, but he glanced around and appeared to deliberately drag it down, leaning closer to Richard. "But you're Grady Porter's Richard. You can't whore yourself to some fat bastard for an alliance. It's not right."

"He's not that bad. But what's it matter anyway? Grady's dead. So I either go without forever or I make do. There isn't another Grady out there, so I'm never going to care about anyone again."

"It's not…right." It was Denny's turn to slump back in his chair, shaking his head.

"What's not right is Grady being dead, but there's not a lot I can do about that either," Richard said quietly. "Just…I don't know anything. Grady wasn't even that keen on being touched, you know, that way, sexually. I know nothing. I can't even read subtext although sometimes I know there is one. I don't know what's the right kind of touching and what's seedy. I've watched porn films but I don't get what's normal and what's way-out-there perverted. When I see one, I'm either wondering if they're slaves and if so, how do we get them free or I'm thinking about the mechanics or…shit." He smoothed his hands over his face, breathing deeply.

"I don't want to do anything without understanding what's happening, what's expected. Plus I don't want Simms, or anyone else, knowing just how innocent and vulnerable I am. I know it's going to take a while for me to learn, but I don't want to feel pressured or rushed and I don't just want to know how to stick what where. I want to know about subtleties and what's right. I don't want to ask a whore who's working other clients so..." Richard hitched a shoulder, looking expectantly at Denny. "I'm asking you."

"Why me?"

"Why not?" Richard didn't look away. "I heard Paxman had caught somebody. I checked around. Word is you know what you're doing and you can help me with my problem. You need a break and I can help." He shrugged again. "You're away from him no matter what happens. I'm hoping that if I help you, you'll be discreet about our deal. Not so much for my sake, but because I don't want anybody saying stuff about Grady. He's too important."

"So it's me because I was in the right circumstances at the right time?"

"Or the wrong ones, depending how you look at it. There's no pressure here. The only thing I ask is you protect Grady's reputation. The rest is up to you. Walk away now if you want. I'll still get you your papers, point you in the right direction, same as I would for any ex-slave."

Denny drummed his fingers on the table and stared at Richard's face for a long while before he gave a curt, brief nod. "All right, I'll do it. I'll give you some time. I'll teach you everything I know and I won't fuck anybody else. I'll keep you clean and tell you what's appropriate. I just hope to God you know what you're doing."

"Thank you." Richard nodded back. "And so do I."

Chapter Two

The ride back to Richard's house was mostly made in silence but, Richard thought, it was a simple, amiable silence. No one was trying to prove a point, no one had to pretend.

The house was on the outskirts of town. It was nothing special, just a single-story structure set in a large area of rough land with a ramshackle outbuilding nearby. Richard knew the place had a rundown feel to it but everything was clean, if basic. The only thing that looked new was the high security gate barring the entrance to the drive. Denny turned to Richard and raised an eyebrow when he saw it.

Richard shrugged. "I like to be able to close both eyes when I go to sleep."

"And you need protection like that to do it?"

"I don't suppose I do anymore, not really. But old habits die hard and there're a lot of people out there who still don't exactly like me. A lot of people who don't like what we took away from them." He knew that feelings almost certainly went a lot stronger than 'don't like' when it came to him and the freedom movement.

"Is this yours and Grady's house?" Denny changed the subject as Richard got back in the car after locking the gate behind them.

"No, he died before we were safe enough to stay anywhere long. Before that we lived wherever we could." Richard led the way inside, flicking on lights as he went, pointing out rooms as he passed. It was much the same as outside, dirt-free but spartan. There was a living room, bedroom, kitchen, and bathroom. Small, but enough for his needs.

"That's nice," Denny said, pointing to the single framed photograph on the wall in the living room.

It showed Grady and Richard, arms around each other's shoulders, Grady's hand on Richard's chest, smiling at one another. Richard loved the way his dark hair contrasted with Grady's blond. But their looks were a match for the other, although Grady was smaller, softer, and maybe a bit more feminine. He thought they looked relaxed and in love, secure in themselves and comfortable around others. In the background there were people from the freedom movement. But the photo hadn't been taken at one of the big rallies—it had been a small, informal gathering.

"You both seem..." Denny hesitated, as though searching for the right word. "Happy."

"We were. That was a good day." Richard touched the frame, straightening it unnecessarily and running his thumb over Grady's leg.

"How long have you been living here?" Denny asked.

"I bought it a couple of years ago. I thought I ought to have a place but... It's never felt much like home."

"Is that why you haven't moved your stuff in?" Denny glanced around at the few possessions scattered about.

"What do you mean—?" Richard started to say, but broke off with a grin. "This is all I've got. Keeping stuff was pretty hard going when you had to suddenly up and move in the middle of the night because the security police were on your tail. Shit, sorry, I didn't think. Did you want to collect your things before we came here?"

Denny shook his head. "I haven't got much and none of it's worth keeping. To be honest, it's probably all been stolen now anyway. There's nowhere to hide anything on the street."

Richard felt the urge to say sorry again. He knew exactly what Denny meant and the movement should have done more to protect him. They'd fucked up but, he supposed, at least they'd tried, and still were.

The silence lengthened as they stood looking at each other across the sofa, and things almost started to get awkward.

"So what do you want to do now? Do you want anything else to eat or drink or are you going to get cleaned up right away?" Richard said.

"Do I stink that bad?" Denny grinned.

Richard thought it looked right on him. Here was a guy that was supposed to be happy, only the world had conspired against him. "Yeah, a bit." Richard found himself grinning back.

"How bad? One bar of soap or two?"

"At least three, I'd say. Oh, and a couple of bottles of shampoo."

Denny's laugh barked out of him, surprising Richard. "You say the sweetest things."

"Hey, man, I've been there. Once went four months without my skin seeing water."

"At least you can't smell yourself after a while," Denny said. "Bathroom this way, right?" He pointed at a door. "What do you reckon? Bath first to soak the dirt off then a shower?"

"I'd go the other way round. Rinse the worst off and then soak the ground-in stuff. I'll bring you some more soap and a towel."

"Thanks."

Richard watched as Denny walked away, leaving the bathroom door open behind him. What was he doing? Had he gone totally crazy or was he just preparing himself for every eventuality, like Grady had always told him to? After Grady's death he hadn't wanted anyone near him, not even a consoling arm or a shoulder to cry on. It wasn't that a physical touch felt like a betrayal, more that he simply couldn't stand the thought. He'd hurt that bad. Now? Now he could be touched, agreed it was probably time to move on, but the idea of sex, of intimacy with anyone else...?

No. He had to separate the two. That was the only way. Sex with someone else? Yes, he could handle that. He didn't especially need it but he could do it. Intimacy? That would always be Grady's. He could do one without the other.

When he went into the bathroom with towels and extra soap, Denny was in the shower, the small cubicle full of steam. "How you doing?" Richard called out.

"I don't seem to have made much headway. Although I've used all your shampoo already and I think I might have clogged up the drain. Man, I didn't even realize how dirty I was."

"Keep going. You'll get there and I have more shampoo." He gathered up the pile of Denny's clothes then took them out to the kitchen.

On closer inspection there really wasn't a lot of hope for any of Denny's stuff. What wasn't torn or worn through was, as Richard had suspected, held together by dirt. There were even a few insects, the kind Richard had hoped he'd never have to see again, living in the lining. Maybe in other circumstances they weren't completely hopeless, but Richard couldn't see the point in trying to save them.

"Denny," he shouted, "can I just dump all this stuff and buy you some new in the morning?"

"What?" Denny called back.

"Can I...?" Pointless. Richard went back to the bathroom. "Can I throw your clothes away and we'll get some more tomorrow? There are unidentified life forms living in the dirt."

"Do whatever you like," Denny said. "Look." He was sitting up in the old claw-footed enamel bath, holding out his arm. Pink skin showed where he'd just rubbed it with the bar of soap. "I'm getting clean at last. Real God's honest clean skin. I don't want any dirty clothes touching me after all this hard work."

"You look...better," Richard admitted. "Although you've still got a long way to go."

"I know. I've been scrubbing at my nails. I ruined your nail brush, sorry." He grinned, looking anything but sorry.

"It's okay, I've got another." Richard smiled gently in return. "But what the hell are you going to do with your hair?"

"Ah, well." Denny poked at the pile of bubbles on his head. "I was hoping I could soak it clean but it doesn't seem to be working. I might have to cut some of it off."

"Some?"

"I'm not getting rid of it all. That'd be cruel to the nits. They'd have nowhere to live."

"The nits?" Richard's eyes widened.

Then Denny started to laugh, a small rumble that soon turned into a full-throated, chest-shaking roar. Next thing Richard knew he was laughing right along with him. On and on it went, on both sides of the room, the pair of them were doubled over with tears running down their faces. Richard couldn't remember the last time he'd laughed like that, with such abandon.

And all over nits? Fucking amazing.

"Man, I'm never going to get clean." Denny snorted. "I've still got a tide mark around my neck even though I've already scrubbed it."

"More hot water, more soap," Richard ordered, searching through a cupboard. "We're not going to be beaten by a bit of dirt." He poured half a bottle of shampoo onto Denny's head.

"I'll smell good if nothing else," Denny spluttered, rubbing the soap in.

Richard watched as he disappeared under the water to rinse it off. Not done yet but certainly better.

Denny came up and lay back, fingers running through his hair. "Richard," he said quietly, less confident. "I don't think I'm joking about the nits."

Richard went back to the cupboard, returning with another bottle. "Here, use this. This is the best stuff for killing the bastards. Trust me, I know."

"You keep a supply ready?"

"It got to be a habit." Richard shrugged.

Richard found more soap and another nail brush as Denny rubbed in the lotion, then went back to scrubbing while they waited for it to work. Then they spent a comfortable but hushed twenty minutes combing out the dead bodies of the insects. It was a job Richard had done many, many times before but not one he thought he'd have to do again. In a strange way it was soothing, almost calming, and felt ridiculously normal. When they were finished he left Denny to shower off the lotion and returned to the kitchen. He poured two shots of whiskey then left one on the opposite side of the table from where he sat.

A few minutes later Denny appeared, barefoot and wearing Richard's bathrobe, rubbing his hair with a towel.

"Do you want…?" Richard nodded toward the glass as Denny sat down.

"Yeah," Denny said. He sniffed at the liquid before drinking most of it straight off and shivering. "Been a very long time since I've had any hard stuff," he added with feeling.

"Are you all right?"

Denny nodded. "I'm pretty clean, even if I have gone wrinkly. It feels, I don't know, good. Better." He turned his hands over, showing deep grooves and ridges on his fingers.

"You'll live." Richard studied Denny's palms and swallowed the last of his liquor before pouring himself another small measure.

They sat companionably for a while, nursing their drinks, as the darkness outside the window soothed them into easy breathing and relaxed muscles.

"Bed?" Denny asked eventually, glancing over at Richard almost curiously.

Richard pressed his lips together and looked straight back. What was he doing? Had he gone stark staring mad? He was going to drive himself crazy at this rate. What was it Grady had always said? 'Make a decision and stick to it.' Stick to it. It was good advice but had he thought this through enough? What would Grady have made of his actions? What if…?

Denny made the decision for him, getting up and turning off the light as he headed toward the bedroom. Richard licked the last taste of whiskey from his lips, then took a deep breath, and followed. Make a decision and stick to it. He purposely put their glasses in the sink, made a quick visit to the bathroom, checked to make sure the doors were locked, then turned off the hall light.

He strode firmly toward the bedroom but suddenly stopped in the doorway, resting his hand on the frame. "Denny," he said softly, his gaze fixed on the other man's face. He hesitated for a moment, organizing his thoughts. If he had to be sure about this, he wasn't the only one. "You don't have to do this. I'm not going to throw you out tonight. I'll sort out your papers and you can stay here until I find you somewhere else. Then I'll help you get started in whatever you want. You really don't have to do this."

Denny stood by the side of the bed, the edge of the bathrobe between his fingers. The stillness had settled back over him, the type Richard always associated with slaves. Waiting for whatever was going to happen, powerless to control anything. It had started to slip in the restaurant as they'd talked and Richard had got to see the man hidden underneath, had almost got used to him. Now it was back.

"Don't sell yourself short," Richard said. "You have a chance now to be whatever you want. You have a clean slate, take it. I'm sorry we let you down before. I won't do it again."

Still Denny simply stood then, slowly, the stillness lifted and the man that had laughed so hard in the bath was back. "I'm going to do this. I want to do this."

"But you don't have to. You can—" Richard started.

"And that's the whole point," Denny interrupted. "I don't have to and you made that possible. Yeah, freedom might have been a little late in reaching me but I know there were enough people a lot worse off than I was. I'm free now and I didn't do a damned thing to earn it. If helping you out is my contribution then it's a fucking easy one, and one I really don't mind doing."

"But—" Richard tried again.

"Shut up." Denny grinned, lazy and smooth. "Now get your ass into bed."

Richard's mouth went dry and he wondered all over again what the hell he was doing.

Looking confident, standing tall, Denny untied the robe, let it fall from his shoulders, and slid into bed. Absently Richard noticed that Denny was already half-hard. Richard exhaled slowly then pulled off his boots and socks, pushing his jeans down to fall on top of them before dragging his T-shirt up over his head then reaching for the covers.

"Trust me. You'll need to take those off as well." Denny nodded at his boxers.

Dutifully Richard pulled them off, trying hard not to think about the way his traitorous blood was heading toward his cock. He sat up in bed and methodically took off his watch, turning to place it carefully on the nightstand. He didn't want anyone getting scratched and... He heard Denny hitch in a breath of surprise as

31

gentle fingertips traced along a scar on his back. Denny outlined another and another, ghosting over the uneven ridges. "How did you get all these?"

The scars crossed Richard's broad shoulders, marring the skin over bone, muscle and tendon, down the length and curve of his back to his tailbone. Deep in a couple of places, lighter elsewhere, not covering everywhere, but enough. More than anyone should have. They criss-crossed and ran parallel in a parody of a pattern.

"Most of them are from early on, when the police thought of us more as plain criminals than a real political threat. I got caught a few times, beaten, but no worse than a lot of people went through. It would have been different had it happened later on, when they were really trying to hunt us down. I wouldn't have got away with a few scars then. I got lucky."

"Lucky?" Denny said as Richard felt him rub across a slanted, wide pockmark. "That doesn't look lucky."

"That was more recent. I was stabbed by someone who tried to turn us in. But we got him in the end."

"I never got hurt like this, not ever. Not enough to leave scars."

"Then you were lucky. A lot were hurt."

"Grady?"

"Yeah."

"I'm sorry for both of you." Denny laid the whole of his hand flat between Richard's shoulder blades.

"I'm sorry for us all."

Denny smoothed his palm over and around, and Richard found himself being pulled back and pressed into the pillow with a hand on his chest. Denny stroked over his biceps and nipple, down to his elbow and waist, over the scar etched into his arm, the small marks on his chest. "The big difference between you and me is that you could have walked away. You had a choice. You could have, but didn't. Don't be sorry now. Tonight is about the present, the future."

Richard's breath stuttered in his chest as Denny leaned in slowly and pressed their lips together. It was soft at first, gentle kisses dropped across his mouth. Then Denny slid his tongue out, tracing the outline of Richard's lips as he curled his hands around Richard's neck and jaw.

"I'm not a girl," Richard breathed when Denny lessened the pressure. "You don't have to treat me like one."

Denny pulled back and grinned, warm and wicked. "Neither am I." Then he was pushing in harder, dirtier, angling his head so their noses didn't bump and their mouths fit more tightly.

Richard closed his eyes, bit back a groan, and opened up to the kiss, lapping into Denny's mouth, sliding over his tongue. He felt Denny's cock forced up against his hip, big and hard. Felt Denny's hands slipping over his flesh, rubbing with just the right touch to make his skin tingle. He rose up into the kiss, giving as good as he got, but...his hands. What was he supposed to do with his hands? He dug his fingers into the mattress, arms outstretched. Should he hang onto Denny? If so, where? His arms, shoulders, hips, hair? Grady hated hands in his hair, pressure on his head... *Grady. Grady, Grady, Grady. Fuck it, stop that.* He had no business thinking about Grady now but...

As if on cue, Denny grabbed one of Richard's hands, pulling it up and placing it on his head. Richard huffed a laugh into Denny's mouth and compromised. He curled his fingers around Denny's neck as he pushed his tongue in for more, angling his head so he could reach deeper.

"Jesus shit," Denny said when he eased back for air a good while later. "You sure weren't lying when you said you'd done a lot of kissing. Man, you're good." He licked over his own puffy lips.

"Thank you, I think." Richard wasn't sure what else to say to that. Wasn't sure what he thought about it.

"Ready to take this a bit further?"

"I...I don't know. I guess I'm leaving myself in your capable hands."

"And mouth." Denny grinned, kissing Richard again before moving to nip at his jaw and along his neck. Slowly, methodically, he worked his way down Richard's body with his hands and mouth as Richard blinked up into nothing, trying hard not to think.

Denny pushed Richard's thighs apart, sliding easily between them, running his hands up to press them farther open. He wet his lips before blowing a stream of air along Richard's cock then tugging at a few hairs around the base with his teeth. The muscles in Richard's belly hitched and tensed in response. "You have been blown before, right?"

"Y-yeah," Richard stuttered. "A few times, but it's been a long while. A very long while."

"No worries. It's like riding a bike," Denny said confidently. "You'll soon remember."

He started slow and easy, sucking on the tip, lapping up the shaft. Richard could feel the confidence in every one of Denny's self-assured skills as his hands rested on Richard's hips, ready to hold him down. But they weren't needed. Richard kept himself stretched tight, under control. Denny upped the pace, drawing the length down, bobbing his head ruthlessly, using his teeth just a bit more. Richard shifted his hands from Denny's head. One went to the bed, pulling a death grip on the spindle of the headboard above him, the other dragging at the sheet. And yet his hips stayed still, pinned to the bed.

"That's not right." Denny whispered the words against Richard's skin as he brushed his thumbs in arcs across his static hips. "Got to do something about that."

As Denny opened his throat a little and let the tip slide down, Richard caught his breath with a loud gulp. His thighs shook but he didn't move. Denny glanced up at him and tried it again, with the same result. Richard couldn't help his sharp intake of breath or his shaking belly muscles but he stayed the movement of his hips. Again and the shaking got more noticeable but he didn't move. A harder suck, a press with Denny's tongue, but he kept his body still.

Shaking his head, Denny pulled off, looking up along the body laid out on the bed. "You can move, man, you should. You don't have to lay there like a dead jellyfish, holding back all the time. Thrust up."

"I..." Richard's voice shook.

"Come on, fuck my mouth. It'll feel good for both of us."

"I can't... I could never... He..." Richard could hear his voice threatening to crack.

"Grady. Oh fuck, of course. You trained yourself not to move or push," Denny said. "Okay, don't worry." He smoothed a reassuring hand up Richard's thigh, reassessing quickly. "We'll keep that for another lesson. But relax. You'll never enjoy yourself unless you relax. I'm not going to hurt you and you sure as hell aren't going to hurt me. Now relax."

Denny went back to turning Richard's brains to mush and Richard did his damnedest to comply with the instruction.

Slip and suck, cheeks hollowing, hand working at his balls. Richard knew he didn't stand a chance of holding on. Denny was just too good at this. One minute Richard was huffing and puffing, body wriggling, chest rising and falling even if his hips didn't, hands as far away from Denny as he could get them. The next they were dug deep in Denny's hair, not pressing and pushing, but pulling. Pulling Denny off and away.

"Off, off," Richard panted. "Get out of the way, I'm gonna…"

"So?" Denny twisted, trying to free himself from Richard's grip and get his mouth back in place. "That's the idea."

"No, you have to move. I can't help it, I'm going to come."

Richard heard the realization in Denny's sudden intake of air.

Denny rubbed his fingers across the skin on Richard's hips, not letting go but not holding. Massaging in firm, reassuring strokes, his chin resting on Richard's inner thigh. "Listen to me. You want to learn the rules — well, I'm telling you. The etiquette when someone's blowing you is that you let them know when you're about to come, at least the first few times you're together, until you know what works for them. Then, whether a guy swallows, spits, or pulls off before it happens is up to them. Some like to spit it back over you, some like getting a face full, some don't want anything to do with it. Me, I want to know what you taste like. That's my decision. I know what I like, I know there's no pressure, and you don't get to argue, okay?"

"But…"

"You don't get to argue."

Richard stared up at the ceiling for a moment, his chest heaving. Fuck, none of this was going to be easy. He'd thought he'd known nothing, but he was wrong, he knew less than that. He had things all backwards and upside down and…

"Richard." Denny pressed on his hips again. "Stop thinking and let it happen."

Richard did and it was all over unsurprisingly quickly. A few hard sucks, a hand on his balls, and Richard was coming and calling out in breathy, mumbled shivers. Denny swallowed with ease, drawing Richard gently through it, until he was sated and breathing more quietly.

Denny let Richard's cock slip from his mouth, patted him once on the thigh, then pulled himself up next to him. "All right?"

"Yeah, I…" Richard ran a hand over his face. "I guess I should say thank you."

"Only if you're a complete asshole." Denny grinned. "Want to taste yourself?"

"Oh, that's gross." Richard wrinkled his nose.

"Go on, you know you want to."

Denny kissed him without waiting for an answer and Richard found he didn't really mind.

"Do I get the reverse lesson now?" Richard asked, hitching his hip against Denny's hard cock.

"Only if you feel like it," Denny said. "No pressure."

"I feel like it." Richard heaved himself up with an effort.

Denny flopped over then inched backward until he was sitting with his back against the headboard, spreading his legs wide and looking down. "You done this before?"

"Yeah." Richard nodded, settling himself between Denny's thighs, eyes right in line with his cock. "More than I've had it done to me. But, man, I've never got this close to one this size before."

"Don't worry, just take what you can. I'm not going to ram it down your throat."

"For which I will be everlastingly grateful," Richard said, slicking his lips then sliding them over the tip. He tested out the taste with his tongue, applying a little pressure here, a little less there, hand gentle at the base. Not Grady, but it was okay.

Denny stroked a hand over a scar on Richard's shoulder. "Normally, when someone is doing this to me, I like to close my eyes, let my mind wander and wallow in the sensations," he said quietly. "But with you…with you I want to watch. Watch the way you study me with such intent, carefully planning your next move, thinking about what you're doing as though it really matters if you get it right." He curled a hand around Richard's face, fingers tracing under his eye, around his ear.

"Shut up." Richard huffed out a laugh but took the touch as a sign of approval and went a little deeper. He lapped at the length, stroking his fingers softly in time with his tongue as he looked up for signs of approval and consent.

"You're a nice man, real gentle and considerate. But you need to go a little harder," Denny said in a kind, encouraging tone. "Add a bit more pressure, squeeze me tighter. I can take it."

Again Richard flicked his gaze up, this time questioning.

"I need it a bit harder." Denny stroked Richard's face. "I need the friction. I know what you're used to, but most guys need a bit more."

Richard's hand shook while he stared at Denny.

"You won't hurt me or freak me out, honestly. You just need to learn to go harder."

That's what Richard was here to do, to learn. So okay, he could do this. He pulled himself up, planting one elbow on the mattress for leverage, and sucked harder, cheeks hollowing under the pressure as he matched his hand to the rhythm.

"Oh, man, that's better." Denny groaned, hips rolling forward as he leaned back. "You learned that quick enough and...oh." His cock twitched when Richard accidentally twisted at the tip.

It might have been an accident the first time around, but if Denny reacted like that, Richard would make sure it wasn't one the next time. Damned right he could learn fast.

"Touch me," Denny said, breathy and panting. "Not lightly. Rub over my belly, squeeze my balls, something. You are allowed to touch me and...oh fuck." Richard sucked again and Denny huffed.

Richard kept one hand on Denny's dick as he ran the other up his thigh and over his hard belly until a fingertip caught at his nipple and Denny actually gasped. Richard would remember that. He flicked it once, feeling Denny jump under him. Then he reached down to Denny's balls, trying to squeeze in time with his other hand and his mouth and, fuck, that took coordination and concentration and...too late.

If he'd been sensible he would have thought beforehand whether he wanted to spit, swallow, or get out of the way. But he hadn't been, and now it was too late, and...

He'd always swallowed with Grady. Doing the same with Denny seemed natural. He rolled over, wiping his mouth with the back of his hand while Denny made odd groaning sounds as he slipped down the bed. They lay side by side, shoulders pressed together. Not intimate but...comfortable. Yeah, Richard thought, comfortable and easy were good words to describe them.

"So." Denny exhaled noisily. "Lesson one went well, don't you think?" He turned his head to look across at Richard.

"Yeah, I think." Richard grinned, just a gentle smile but meaning it. "Yeah, it went well."

"And lesson two won't be anywhere near as scary?"

"I wasn't scared," Richard hit back.

"Sure you were. You'd have been quaking in your boots, if you had any on."

"Not quaking, but maybe a little..."

"Petrified," Denny finished for him.

"Maybe a little nervous. I thought you'd think I was a total idiot."

"Nah." Denny patted his thigh. "I think you're sweet."

"Oh, that's totally worse. I'd rather be petrified than sweet." Richard laughed.

"Idiot." Denny left his hand where it was.

They fell quiet again, the limited light from the bedside lamp keeping out the rest of the world as though it didn't exist. Just for now.

"What are you thinking?" Denny asked after a long while.

"Nothing." Richard shrugged.

"What," Denny prompted softly, "about Grady? Don't feel guilty. If he was half the man I think he was, he'd want you to move on."

"I wasn't. I... I'm sure about him. He was a good man. He'd want the best for me."

"So you were just remembering him?"

"No," Richard said easily. "I wasn't thinking about him at all. Actually, I was thinking about you."

"Me?"

"I was just wondering." He looked at Denny. "Have you ever had sex just because you wanted to?"

"Yeah," Denny said, sounding surprised at the question. "I did it when I had to but that left a lot of time. No one knew what you got up to when you were locked up for the night. I don't think they cared as long as I could get it up when they wanted. I think they had an idea that if I got laid regularly it kept me more docile."

"Did you do it with anyone you cared about?"

Denny took a moment to think. "There were a few people I cared for, couple of girls, some more guys. Other slaves that were either owned by the same people or living in for some reason."

"Anyone you loved?"

"You learned not to love." Denny's face closed up.

"I'm sorry." Richard slid a hand over to cup Denny's elbow. "I shouldn't have asked."

"Sure you should." Denny rolled over onto his side, facing Richard, the lines of tension easing and expression returning to his eyes. "There was an old woman living at the place when I first got sold there, a slave, she'd been there for years. I was only a kid. I'd been taken from my mom so long before I couldn't really remember her even then, and I never knew any of my other family. I'd been sold around factories and places, never stayed anywhere long enough to get attached to anyone, but then I met Lily. She sort of took me under her wing, taught me how to keep my head down but keep my soul. Do you know what I mean?"

Richard nodded. To keep that little bit that made you who you were, to not let the owners even know it was there. He knew.

"She kept me sane. Taught me to cry and let it out and I loved her."

"What happened?"

"Nothing dramatic. She was there in the morning, gone by lunch. Sold on when she was too old for heavy work. I heard from someone else she was in a good place, lived okay and died peacefully. But I never saw her again and it broke my heart. I made sure I never loved anyone again after that."

"I'm s—"

"If you say you're sorry again I'll kick you in the balls," Denny interrupted with a smile. "It wasn't your fault."

"Okay, warning duly noted, but...okay." Richard returned the smile.

"Anything else you want to know about me?" Denny asked, open and easy as he slid a hand under his face.

"Yeah." Richard regarded him carefully. "You're not how I thought you'd be. When most slaves first get freedom they're wary, watchful, always on their guard. You're not. You've opened up a lot quicker than I expected. You smile and laugh. I guess I'm just surprised."

He watched as Denny thought about it. "I haven't technically been a slave for a while. Not until Paxman caught me two days ago."

"But you haven't really been free."

Again Denny seemed to consider things. "It's... Slaves always have two kinds of lives, one where they're careful and quiet around owners, the other more open, when they're alone. You learn the difference and how to move between the two quickly or you don't get any life of your own."

"And you don't think of me like an owner?"

"No, but it's more than that." Denny chewed on the side of his mouth for a moment. "It's you. You're different, you're... Fuck it, you're Grady Porter's Richard, for God's sake. But it's even more than that. You treated me differently, right from the start. I'm not a slave to you or an ex-slave or an anything. I'm just a guy, just Denny."

"I'm glad you think that."

Denny shrugged. "Some people like slaves, some people like the idea of ex-slaves. It turns them on. I've met both. But you, it's like you don't do categories. Everyone has to prove themselves just as people."

"I hope that's a good thing."

"Yeah, it is. But you're different than what I expected as well."

"Different how?"

"At the restaurant you were all uptight, like you were holding yourself in." Denny's gaze fell heavily on Richard. "Now that you're relaxed, you've opened up as well. Even if you have trouble doing it during sex."

It was Richard's turn to consider things. "There are a few people who know what I'm really like. Most of them have known me a very long time and they understand. The rest of the world has an idea of me. I'm Grady's right-hand man. I'm not the leader he was but I'm not to be messed with. In reality, I don't let people in. It's too hard after what we went through. But I guess with you, I told you up front. You know how naïve I am in some things. I've got nothing else as important as that to hide."

"It makes it easier, doesn't it, having everything out there. You know about slaves, know I was one, but it doesn't matter to you. I know about you and again, what's it really matter? It just makes things easy between us."

"It does," Richard agreed. "And I am pleased you don't think I'm a total moron, although I think 'sweet' is kind of harsh."

Denny laughed. "You're doing all right, Grady Porter's Richard."

Richard smiled and pushed at Denny's shoulder halfheartedly, rolling him over onto his back. "Go to sleep, you fucking idiot, before you say something really stupid."

"Do you want me to stay here or go somewhere else?" Denny carried on laughing but it didn't quite reach his eyes anymore.

"There isn't anywhere else in this place," Richard said. "Unless you like the sofa. Although I figure, with your size, that'd get uncomfortable really quick."

"You sure?" Denny checked.

"Go to sleep," Richard said again, and this time Denny nodded and did as he'd been told.

* * * *

Richard woke late in the night when it was dark and silent. It took him a moment to remember all that had happened, then to realize he had an arm looped over Denny's waist. Was that part of the deal? Touching after sex? After the lesson, as Denny had called it. He wasn't sure, didn't understand the rules of his own arrangement. He turned over onto his side, his back to Denny, and waited for sleep to claim him again.

He'd been unfaithful to Grady.

The thought was there, sudden and bright. For the first time in his life he'd had sexual contact with someone other than Grady and… Yeah, there was a pang of something and the muscles in his belly tightened. But it wasn't guilt. Maybe it was regret, but whatever it was, he was okay with it.

When the birds were starting to sing outside, he woke again. He was lying on his stomach at the edge of the bed, one arm hanging off, the fingers starting to tingle. Denny was all but spooned in behind him, breath warm on his neck.

He went back to sleep.

Chapter Three

When Denny woke the next morning, the bed was already empty and he could hear the water running in the bathroom. He stretched, luxuriating in the soft mattress, clean sheets, and the thought of more food. Damned lucky, that's what he was. After all, what more could a man want?

His cock twitched between his legs and he grinned. A hot shower and Richard's mouth? Life really didn't get much better, not for someone like him. He scrambled out of bed, dick already hard as he strode toward the bathroom. Pulling open the door of the small cubicle, he laughed at Richard's surprised squeak. "Consider lesson two a revision of lesson one," he said as he pressed Richard up against the wall and closed the door behind him. "It's my chance, as your teacher, to see how much you've remembered."

Turned out Richard remembered an awful lot. The things he could do with his mouth were pretty amazing. But that wasn't all there was to sex.

Okay, so maybe Denny knew that they had to take things slow and that Richard wasn't going to change the habits of a lifetime overnight. But, shit, the guy still wouldn't touch him unless he was explicitly instructed to do so. Richard held himself in check all the time, every reaction squashed down behind a wall of self-control that was as thick and strong as ever. Unsure how to touch. Even less sure how to be touched.

This was going to take some working on.

At breakfast, Denny couldn't help a little laugh as Richard sat with his hair mussed, looking stunned while he ate his toast. "You all right, man?"

"I..." Richard sighed. "I'm not used to this much sex or an orgasm that hit so, so...hard."

Denny plowed through bacon, eggs, sausages, toast and the last of the cereal. He hadn't had this much sex in a while either, but it had a different effect on him. "So what's the plan for today?" he asked. "Anything you have to do or need me to do?"

Richard seemed to shake himself awake. "Well, we'll start on your papers first. They'll take a few hours at least. While they're being sorted we'd better get some groceries. With the amount you eat I can't have anything left."

"Sorry." Denny smiled, not sounding it at all.

"And clothes. We need to get you some clothes."

"What do I wear while we're getting them? You threw my things away and I can't exactly go out in your bathrobe." He pulled at the blue and green striped garment he was wearing.

"You'll have to..." Richard looked him up and down. "Shit, you'll have to be a total dork with pants halfway up your legs in my stuff. There's nothing else for it."

"I promise to try and not rip anything." Denny wiped his hands on the robe. "I'm ready."

* * * *

The new government's office was crowded when they arrived, but one look at Richard and they were ushered almost reverentially to a small room. Richard explained what he wanted and said they'd be back in a few hours to collect the new papers. The woman behind the desk seemed as though she was about to protest, but a quick glance from Richard stopped her. Denny thought being with one of the uprising's leaders had its advantages.

Back outside, Richard studied Denny in the too-tight jacket and the completely ridiculous sweatpants. "Clothes next. Being with you is ruining whatever meager street credibility I ever had."

Denny didn't argue as he followed Richard into a large store selling men's clothing. They looked around at the racks.

"What do you like?" Richard asked.

"I don't know." Denny touched the sleeve of a red leather jacket. "Never had a choice before. I wore what I was told."

"I'm not telling you, so you'd better start deciding." Richard folded his arms over his chest and watched while Denny was given a whole new pleasure.

An hour later he wasn't quite so sure it was such a pleasure.

"Are you sure you want snakeskin cowboy boots and the jacket with the tassels hanging from the arms?" Richard asked.

"You don't like them?"

"Doesn't matter if I like them. Are you sure you do?"

Denny held up the jacket. "I think it's stylish."

"Not the word I'd use, but if you like it put it in the basket. Now underwear. You've got to have underwear because you're not wearing mine again. That's too gross."

Another hour and a half later and they were finally done. Denny had several pairs of jeans plus one good pair of pants. Richard insisted everyone needed one good pair. T-shirts, shirts, socks, underwear, sweatshirts, sports shoes, and lace-up boots were all stashed in the basket. He'd given up on the cowboy ones, although he did still have the tasseled jacket. Richard had persuaded him to add another plain jacket. Just in case, he said.

Denny watched as the bill racked up, staying silent while Richard paid. "That was an awful lot of money, wasn't it?" he asked when they walked away.

"It's okay."

"You got money like that? I mean, to just blow?"

Richard stopped and looked at him. "I haven't got a lot. Nothing like what some people think I have. You don't get paid fighting the government. But I've got some, enough to get by on at least. We're part of the system now so we get something like a wage or an allowance. I've never really had anything to spend it on before."

"Apart from buying slaves their freedom?"

"Sort of," Richard said. "Now go and get changed. I am not walking around a supermarket with you dressed like that."

Denny laughed and took a bag from Richard's hand. "Can we get something to eat first? I'm starving. Oh," he called back over his shoulder as he headed toward a cubicle. "Do you want your boxers back before or after they're washed?"

"I don't want them back at all." Richard waved a hand as though trying to shoo the idea away and Denny laughed again.

In the supermarket Denny was like a kid in a candy store. His eyes widened as Richard dropped bags and cans of food into the cart, even though he'd only just eaten. But it was the cookie and cake aisle that made him glow, especially when Richard told him to pick what he liked. Denny started trying to hide them after he added the fourth package. He couldn't help it, he felt like he was being greedy.

Denny was gazing longingly at the fresh meat counter when Richard came over. "Can you cook?" he asked.

"Yeah, it was one of my jobs."

"You want steak for dinner tonight?" Richard pointed at two huge hunks of meat and the attendant started to wrap them up.

"For me? I've never had steak like that before. It wasn't given to us."

"But can you cook it? Because I can't manage a damned thing without burning it."

"Sure I can. I did it for the owners but..."

"Then we'll have steak tonight."

"Can you afford all this?" Denny had to ask again.

"Not every day but it won't hurt once in a while." Richard shrugged. "Now what do you want to do next? Get your brands removed or see if your papers are ready?"

Denny didn't know what he wanted. Today was altogether too fucking much to contemplate.

* * * *

Denny sat at the table and just stared at his steak. They said anticipation was half the pleasure but he couldn't stand the idea of spoiling it, of cutting into it and then it'd be gone and he wouldn't have it to look at anymore and…

"If you don't want it I'll have it." Richard glanced over at Denny's plate.

"No," Denny said much too quickly. Old habits died hard and he wasn't about to let this beauty out of his sight, let alone off his plate. "No, it's mine and I'm going to eat it. Once I've thought about it and given it the appreciation it deserves." He looked up and saw Richard smiling gently at him. Denny thought he ought to do it more often. It was better than the weary seriousness his face usually wore. "I just can't quite get my head around the fact it's all mine."

"Don't let it get cold. It's cooked just right. You did good." Richard started eating again. "You want a drink? It'll take the sting out of your hand."

Denny smoothed across the taped bandage on the inside of his wrist. The brands were gone, his marks of ownership, of being nothing but a piece of property. He'd watched as they were burned away, surprised at the way his shoulders had shaken at the thought. Richard had stood behind him and laid a reassuring hand silently on his back. Now his wrist ached a bit, but it was a good ache, one that made him think. The brands were gone and his new papers, all clean and perfect, were propped up on a shelf where he could see them. It had been a hell of a day.

"We left the beer in the car," Richard went on. "So it'll have to be whiskey."

"Yeah, I could manage one." Denny took his first tiny slice, groaning long and loud when he put it in his mouth. "Oh, man, I just died and went to heaven."

"I wish everyone was that easily pleased." Richard gave a rueful grin and carried on eating.

It turned out that they managed more than one drink. By the time they made it to bed they weren't falling-down drunk, but they weren't far from it.

"Lesson number two or three or whatever we're up to," Denny announced, "should be on how to undress a man."

"You only want me to do it because you're incapable."

"You're probably right. Let's do it together."

In the end they succeeded in getting most of their clothes off, but not all, which made their attempted mutual blowjobs all the more difficult. However, guys being guys, they got there in the end.

Denny rolled over and patted Richard's chest. "Okay?"

"Yeah, although I'm not sure what I learned from that lesson."

"You just got to come. Are you really complaining?"

Richard huffed as his face screwed up in thought. "I might not be sure what I learned, but I'm damned sure I don't care."

* * * *

Once more Denny woke to an empty bed, only this time he had a pounding head and a mouth that felt like a desert. He went in search of coffee.

"I was just about to wake you," Richard said when he made it to the kitchen. "I've got to go out. I'll probably be gone all day. Are you going to be okay?"

Denny snorted a laugh and pushed the hair out of his eyes. "I've managed on my own long enough. You don't need to nursemaid me."

"All right." Richard grabbed his jacket. "I left you some money on the fridge. I meant to set you up a bank account yesterday but I forgot."

"I'll make a 'To Do' list." Denny poured coffee, yawned, then slid into a chair.

"Add getting a haircut." Richard stopped by the door. "I've got to take the car but there's a bus from the end of the street or you could walk into town."

"Don't worry, I'm fine." Denny waved a hand vaguely. "Anything you want done?"

Richard shook his head. "Not really. What are you going to do all day?"

"You know what I'd really like? What I've never done before?"

"What?"

"Nothing. I want to sit on my butt in front of the TV, watching what I want and eating crap. All day." Denny couldn't help his slightly embarrassed expression when he looked at Richard. "It's not really what you fought for, is it?"

"Hey, man, if that's what freedom means to you, especially now at the start, then you go for it. Eat whatever you want and enjoy doing nothing."

With that, Richard was gone and Denny settled down to fulfill one of his ambitions.

* * * *

It was a lot later than he'd intended when Richard pulled up in front of the house and got out of the car. He sighed as he walked to the door, feeling tired as hell. Denny was asleep on the sofa with the TV still talking away to itself in the corner. He found a blanket and was just about to cover Denny when he woke up. "You're back," Denny stated the obvious. He blinked himself more awake and scratched at his head.

"Yeah, I didn't think it'd be this late."

"You eaten?"

"You turning into a wife?" Richard smiled.

"Nope, but I did see all the burnt toast you threw in the trash this morning. You weren't lying when you said you couldn't cook."

"I got something while I was out. I'm okay. You had a good day?"

"I had an awesome day." Denny stretched as he stood up. "I did absolutely fucking nothing. I didn't even wash my dishes. Although I will do them tomorrow, promise."

"I'm glad you had a good time. Bored yet?" Richard locked the front door, took off his jacket, then kicked away his shoes.

"Not a chance. One lazy-ass day doesn't make up for years of work." Denny turned off the light then followed him into the bedroom.

"Then you do the same tomorrow. After we sort you out a bank account and a haircut, I've got some stuff to take care of."

"More changing-the-world type stuff?" Denny asked while he undressed. "Like today?"

Richard slipped out of his jeans before sitting the side of the bed. "I don't do any changing-the-world stuff anymore. I just help round the edges. Sometimes I think the war was easy compared to this. At least we knew what we were aiming for then."

"Is it that bad?"

"Not bad." Richard took a deep breath, then exhaled slowly. "It's just... I deliberately bowed out of things once the old government fell. The freedom movement works with the new administration, is part of it. They make sure nothing like the slave system can happen again. They also look after the interests of ex-slaves, helping them move on, making sure they're not discriminated against. But that's not for me. It's all too official, although people keep encouraging me to be more involved than I am."

"What do you want to do?"

Richard shrugged. "I'm tired. Deep down to my bones tired. Tired of everything. I guess I want a little bit of peace and some quiet. I want a chance to remember that I don't have to look over my shoulder all the time anymore, that there isn't really a threat. I've spent so many years running and fighting that I'm a bit like you, I don't want to do anything for a while."

"So why don't you?"

Richard pulled off his sweatshirt then held it in his hands as he looked up at Denny. "Because it's not as easy as that."

"There're still slaves to buy into freedom?"

"Kind of. I don't want part of anything official but I can do some mopping up, checking, sorting out problems. That kind of thing. You prove there's still enough to do."

"Can't you leave it to someone else? Someone who hasn't done so much already?" Denny climbed into bed.

Richard copied him. "I could. But I can't stand the thought there could be someone like Grady hidden away out there, someone still suffering."

"You can't save the whole country. No one can," Denny said softly. "You've done your part."

"I don't do that much anymore. Just things where being 'Grady Porter's Richard' will help. I try to be diplomatic but if that doesn't work I remind people we fought a war for freedom and we're not letting it slip through our fingers now."

"Go easy on yourself, man," Denny said as he turned off the light. He rested a hand on Richard's chest. "You want to…?"

"Not tonight, too tired." Richard sighed. "Unless you want to?"

"Too tired as well." Denny pulled the covers up higher. "I had a busy day doing nothing."

Richard woke only once in the night. Denny's face was pressed into his shoulder, a knee resting on his thigh. He was asleep again before he fully thought about it.

* * * *

A soft hand on his belly, the press of muscle and flesh into his back, fingers slipping and sliding down under his boxers. Richard felt a warm glow start to filter through his bones as he swam toward consciousness, comforting, familiar and…fuck. That wasn't Grady's hand, that wasn't familiar. Grady was dead and… He shot out of bed before his brain had a chance to process any more.

"Hey, where the hell are you going?" Denny asked.

"I…" Only Richard didn't know where he was going or what he was doing. He pushed his hands up through his hair, digging the heels into his eyes as he tried to think. "Nowhere, I…" He rubbed at his face again, his heart going fast as a rabbit's.

"Come back to bed," Denny said, licking at his lips. "Waking a guy up with a hand or blowjob is a really good lesson."

"No." Richard blew out a long breath. "I'm going to take a shower."

"You okay?" Denny asked, head tipping to one side.

"Yeah." Richard deliberately tried to relax his shoulders.

"You sure? I didn't get that wrong, did I?"

"No, I'm fine. Seriously. I just need a shower."

"You want some company?" And was that a bit of uncertainty in Denny's voice?

Richard looked over and gave the best smile he could manage. "Sure, just give me a minute."

Twenty minutes later Denny was on his knees in the shower and Richard remembered again just how skillful his teacher was. Ten minutes after that it was Richard's turn to cope with the hard, wet floor, Denny encouraging him with gentle words.

"That's good, that's so good. Remember, go harder than you think and it's good if you touch me."

Three more minutes and Denny's voice had turned to pleading. "Come on, man, use your hands as well. I like it rough. You don't have to hold yourself away from me. It's good if your shoulder or arm brushes my leg. You're making me feel like you think you'll catch a disease if you touch me."

"I am doing my best here, you know?" Richard said, his voice half-hidden in the rush of the water.

"I know, sorry." Denny curled a hand around Richard's face. "And you're doing real good. I just need a fraction more."

Richard shut up and gave as good as he knew how. A couple of minutes later Denny came with a groan and a garbled comment about Richard's 'touching issues'.

* * * *

"Are you really wearing the tassel jacket to the bank?" Richard asked after breakfast.

"Is it that bad?" Denny primped the collar and adjusted the sleeves.

"It's okay."

"You just hate it?"

"No, no. Hate's the wrong word. I love it." Richard shrugged and raised an eyebrow. "Fuck it, man, you're hot, you wear it. You look good in it, so why not? You're free to wear whatever you want."

"But...?" Denny started. "I can hear the 'but' in your voice."

"You do look a bit like Jon Voight in *Midnight Cowboy*."

"Who? What?"

"It's a film about a...never mind. Come on, haircut first then the bank."

"And then the DVD store. I want to rent this film."

"The shop's shut. Trust me, they're all shut. You don't want to see that film."

* * * *

Richard dropped Denny back at the house at lunchtime before disappearing again, saying he wouldn't be late. He had to meet Harley and do a few jobs but, true to his word, he was back by early evening.

When he got in Denny was just finishing a huge bowl of ice cream, sitting with his feet up on the sofa in front of the TV. "Hi, you want some? This is really awesome." Denny waved his spoon in the air.

"No, I'm good." Richard stood in the middle of the room, coat still on, keys in his hand. "Have you had a good afternoon?"

"Yeah, of course." Denny nodded but he didn't look up and Richard thought he could hear something in his voice.

"Come on, tell me," he encouraged.

"Nothing, really." Denny shook his head. "It's just that…"

"What?"

Denny shrugged. "After you left I made myself a sandwich and sat at the table. I had a beer in one hand, a chocolate bar in the other and even more food spread out in front of me. I suddenly caught sight of myself reflected in the window. I've got a new haircut, new clothes, new papers, a goddamned proper bank account in my name, and a bandage on my wrist where my brand was burned off. I just…"

"Too much?"

"Hell no." Denny snorted but his smile looked a little forced. "But…"

"Fuck?" Richard offered.

"Yeah, exactly. Fuck. That sums it up perfectly. It's all a bit fuck, but in a good way. Do you know what I mean?"

"I know." Richard sucked in a deep breath, holding it for a moment. "Do you want…?"

"What?"

"Do you want to go out for a drink? I mean, if you're bored, stuck in here all the time. Bored and overwhelmed."

"Sure. I'd like that." Denny got up and stretched. "Let me just find my shoes. Are we going anywhere special?"

"No, nothing special."

But as they drove into the center of town Richard got quieter and quieter. By the time they were waved through a gate by two huge security guards, he was hardly speaking. He parked then led the way to some heavy metal doors.

"This isn't an ordinary bar, is it?" Denny asked.

"Not really," Richard admitted. "This is where I hang out. Where people from the movement go. Where my friends are."

"You're introducing me to your friends?" Denny sounded incredulous.

Richard stopped, turning to look at Denny, the car keys tight in his hand. "If there's one thing Grady taught me, it's to do the right thing and to stand by it. I got you out and I sort of gave you a job. Well, now I stand by you. You're living in my house and I'm not going to hide you."

"Are you going to tell them the truth?"

Richard sucked in a breath, then let it out slowly. "I'm not going to lie. Will that do?"

"Okay." Denny nodded. "Your decision," he said, his voice neutral.

Inside there was rock music overlaid with loud conversation. People sat around small tables and at a long bar that ran down one wall. There were pool tables and even a jukebox. The atmosphere was comfortable, friendly, like thousands of other bars across the country. Except half the people here were familiar. Their faces had appeared first in grainy pictures the police had circulated, then later, on the television and in posters celebrating their victory. A few were part of the new government, others had important jobs outside it. All looked battle hardened and capable.

"Fuck," Denny murmured as he glanced round.

"It's all right." Richard was close behind him.

"Fuck. That's fucking Stella Haynes. She was at… And that's fucking Harley whatever his name is. He's like the fucking hardest, meanest son of a bitch going. Fuck, fuck, fuck."

"They're just people. People a lot like you."

"They fucking aren't anything like me."

"Stella used to be a slave. Harley was for a short time as well."

"But…oh, sweet fucking Jesus, is that Detlef Meyer? The leader, the fucking hero savior of us all, the fucking…fuck."

"Calm down." Richard caught hold of his arm, pulling him in. "Detlef's all right. He's a good guy."

"Good guy?" Denny's eyes went impossibly wide as he stared at the small, dark-haired man with glasses. "He's fucking Superman."

"Not quite Superman. He couldn't handle the tights." Richard smiled at Denny's reaction. "But he's about as close as they come. Do you want to meet him?"

"Do I want to meet Detlef Meyer? No, I don't. What could I say to Detlef fucking Meyer?"

"Well, you could try missing out on some of the 'fuckings'. He can swear like a Marine, but it's getting really hard to work out what you're trying to say."

"I…fuck" was all Denny could manage.

"Okay, perhaps we'll leave Detlef for another time." Richard patted his arm. "Let's get you a beer while you recover and then I'll introduce you to a few of the folks here."

Two beers later and Richard had persuaded Denny to talk to a couple of people, convincing him they were, like he'd said, only people and some a lot like him. One older guy had been a slave working on a farm not far from where Denny had been held and Denny seemed easy talking to him. Richard introduced him as a newly released slave and people were interested in his story. Heated debates broke out about why and how they hadn't managed to help everyone earlier. The friendly arguments were the same as with any group of friends. There was a lot of teasing and name calling but it was all supportive and with no heat.

It wasn't until Detlef Meyer walked past on his way out and stopped to hug Richard that Denny visibly paled. Richard put a beer in front of him, told him quietly to stop staring, then placed a reassuring palm on the back of his neck as Detlef shook his hand. Richard even stood guard as Denny refused to use the hand for the next hour.

Richard spent the evening watching Denny trying to process all he'd seen, all the people he'd met, but now it was time to go. He started to collect their things when he heard Denny's sharp intake of breath behind him. Looking around, he saw someone push a little too close into Denny's back.

"Aren't you going to introduce me to your Tassel Boy, Ritchie?"

"Sure." Richard moved nearer. "But he's not my Tassel Boy. He doesn't belong to anyone anymore. This is Denny. And Denny, that fat-assed, can't-control-his-mouth bastard is Harley Ellis, my stupid best friend."

"Harley Ellis is your best friend?" Denny was wide-eyed again.

"Someone had to take him on and I was the only one dumb enough."

Harley ignored Denny. "So if he's not your boy who is he then?"

"He's a friend. Someone who's doing me a favor," Richard said softly.

"A friend?"

"Yeah. Do you have a problem with that?"

"Me? I got no problem. But friends usually do you a favor for free. They don't take money for it. I know how you got him, that you're paying him, what he's meant to be for."

"He's a friend, now be nice," Richard insisted.

Harley turned to Denny and it was obvious Denny had to fight the urge to take a step back. Harley was smaller than Denny and thinner, but he had massive presence. He stuck out his hand and Denny took it. The handshake started off normal enough but then Harley squeezed, pulling Denny in until he could grasp his elbow as well. "You hurt Richard and I will kill you. He's had enough shit to last a lifetime."

"Back off, Harley," Richard said with more than a hint of authority.

Harley stepped away, hands raised. "I'm not out to cause trouble. I'm just stating the facts."

"Okay, now shut up." Richard maneuvered Harley away from Denny and into a corner.

"Have you thought this through properly?" Harley spat the words at Richard, their faces close together.

"I'm trying to protect myself like you keep telling me to," Richard spat back. "If I went off with Simms now he'd —"

"Then don't go off with him or any other asshole. You know you don't have to."

"So I sit in my room and write sad poetry for the rest of my life? Don't I deserve a little more than that?"

"You deserve the world. But try with someone you care about, not just to do the movement a favor."

Richard took a step back, face set hard. "Grady's dead, so I'm kind of fucked on that score."

"Okay, move on. But not like this." Harley shook his head, pushing in closer again. "I know you've been left with problems but you don't buy a fuck toy to get out of them."

Again Richard pulled Harley back, away from Denny. "He isn't a fuck toy and I didn't buy him. I bought his freedom."

"From scum like Paxman? And for this? It's not right."

"It's not so wrong."

"Ritchie." Harley gripped the front of Richard's shirt, almost shaking him. "If you're so proud of it why aren't you telling everyone?"

"It's not a secret, it's just private. Are you going to announce it to the world for me?"

"Of course I'm not, but this isn't what we're about."

"What we're about is giving people a choice. I offered him a job. It was up to him if he took it."

"A sex job?"

"All three of us have done worse." Richard remained defiant.

"And did he really have a choice?"

"Yeah." Richard thrust his chin forward. "I told him I'd still help him out if he said no and you know I keep my word."

Harley dropped his hands from Richard's chest. "But did he? He didn't know you, didn't know what kind of man you are. There's a hell of a lot of scum out there who wouldn't keep their word." He took a couple of steps back, his attention going briefly to Denny. "Think about what you're doing and take care of yourself, man." Then he was gone, back into the throng of people, and Richard was leading Denny outside.

On the way back to the house, Richard glanced over at Denny. "Say something."

"Fuck," Denny groaned, one long, long word that went on for ages.

It caught Richard off guard, making him laugh out loud. "Seems to be your word of the night. Did you hear all that, with Harley?"

"Yeah," Denny admitted.

Richard pulled his old battered car over to the side of the road then switched the engine off, breathing deeply.

"I'm guessing Harley knows everything," Denny said.

"He does." Richard nodded briefly. "He knows me, knows how things were with Grady. He's the only one who does. He also knows I was scared of going into a relationship with Simms unprepared." He shrugged, the gesture encompassing a whole manner of things. "He's my best friend and has been for a long time."

"Now he's looking out for you."

"He is, but I meant what I said. You have a choice, a real choice. I'm offering you a job, I didn't buy you for sex. You can still say no. You were an attractive guy to start with — you've scrubbed up even better. You're intelligent and strong. You have a lot going for you. I'll help you get started somewhere else. That's not an idle offer. Take it if you want it."

Denny sat perfectly still, his gaze fixed on Richard. "No way. I'm hanging onto this job. I'll stay." He nodded firmly. "I'm a man who keeps his word as well."

"You sure?"

"Yeah."

"Okay." Richard exhaled. "Just remember you can change your mind any time you like." He started up the engine again. "And the rest of the night? It was all right?"

"It was…fuck." Denny sighed, deep and loud.

"Back to that again, are you?" Richard couldn't help but laugh.

"What did you expect? I got my hand shaken by Superman and was scared shitless by Harley fucking Ellis. Hell, that was the most…something…evening of my life. It was definitely fucking something, I just don't know what."

"But did you enjoy it?"

"Enjoy? I don't know. Sort of. Bits of it. I'm not quite sure how to react when Stella Haynes is falling-down drunk and I just had my life threatened."

"Told you they were just people, and that wasn't a threat, that was just Harley being protective. He was looking out for you as well."

"Protective?" Denny stared, wide-eyed. "That man would scare the shit out of a grizzly bear. Fuck, he is a grizzly."

"That wasn't scary. You should see him being scary."

"Thanks, but I'll miss that one if you don't mind."

"He's just a good friend. He was to Grady as well. He'll be okay."

Denny shifted in his seat, turning so he could face Richard. "If he's such a good friend, why'd you lie to him?"

"I didn't." Richard looked confused. "I don't lie to him."

"All that stuff you said when you introduced me?"

Richard thought back for a moment. "I told you before we went in that I wasn't going to lie and I didn't."

Denny licked at his lips, looking uneasy. "You called me a friend. Did you mean that?"

"Well, aren't we?"

"I don't know. I've never really had friends before. I always stopped myself before someone got sold on."

"I'm not going anywhere," Richard said gently.

Denny stared out at the road, his lips pressed tightly together. "I…" He shook his head as his chest heaved for a moment. "It was one hell of an evening," he said at last.

"You okay, though?"

"Yeah." Denny nodded. "Let's go home."

When Richard pulled up in front of the house Denny was first out, striding in purposefully. "Are you anywhere near drunk?" he called over his shoulder.

"I'm a bit fuzzy around the edges, why?" But Richard had hardly put a foot through the door before Denny thrust a glass into his hand. It was full to the brim with whiskey.

"Drink it," Denny demanded.

Richard knocked it back before asking once more, "Why?"

"Because…" Denny filled it halfway up again. "I need you off your guard but not falling on your ass."

"And you need me like that because…?" Richard swallowed it down in one again.

"Because I'm hyped up tighter then a coiled rattlesnake and I intend to take it out on your touching issues."

"What?" Richard spluttered, taken by surprise "What 'touching issues'?"

"Your touching issues," Denny dismissed his question.

"Am I going to like this?"

"Sure you will. Now get your clothes off and get on that bed," Denny ordered.

"Oh shit," Richard hissed, damned glad he'd drunk the whiskey. He shed his clothes as he walked toward the bedroom, his mouth suddenly dry.

"Lie on your belly," Denny ordered again.

Wondering when Denny had got naked, Richard did as he'd been told, folding his hands under his face, unexpectedly nervous.

"Now shut your eyes, don't fidget, and most importantly, relax. Think about anything you like except what I'm doing."

That was an order that turned out to be exceptionally hard to follow as Denny used his hands and mouth to touch and taste and explore Richard's body. He started at the ankles, pressing and licking his way across every millimeter of skin, hard enough not to tickle, light enough not to hurt. These were firm, purposeful touches designed to test Richard's limits, and they worked.

Hell, they worked.

At first Richard held himself tight, muscles contracted against the unfamiliar. But slowly, oh so slowly, the alcohol clouding his brain and Denny's determined mouth and fingers had him panting into the pillow.

Inside his thighs, up over rounded cheeks, into the curve of his hips, smoothing across his back. Painstakingly mapping each and every scar in a way that made Richard struggle with himself, humping down into the mattress, rounding his shoulders to rise up against Denny's lips. Why? Why, all of a sudden, had his scars become such sensitive spots? Ones that could send little shivers of…fucking… Richard bit at his lip, harder than was sensible. His scars had never reacted like this before, not with Grady. But then, Grady had usually been there when the scars had been made and that kind of put a damper on…

Denny licked a slow, meticulous trail from under Richard's arm up to nip at his neck, teeth sharp, precise, and deadly effective. Richard sucked in a breath, holding it as he felt the thump, thump, thump of his heart and forgot how to think for a moment. Denny stretched over him to press his face into Richard's hair.

Slowly, carefully, Denny covered him completely. Then back down along his spine, licking, pressing at each and every rounded bone, huge hands running over him, holding him. An open mouth pushed into the hollow at the small of his back, nose against his flesh, hands pulling his cheeks apart, hot breath on him.

"No," Richard huffed, voice small and catching and raw. "I can't, not yet."

Denny immediately seemed to accept it, moving back to Richard's hip, rolling him over onto his back.

"Keep your eyes closed," Denny whispered, his voice as dark and thick as warm molasses. "And just…let me." Again he started at Richard's feet, working each bit of flesh, learning each blemish and scar.

Kisses to Richard's knees, patterns drawn against the direction of the hair, hands finding their way to each and every part. Touches that awakened and excited. Denny push his face to Richard's inner thighs, holding still for a moment, and Richard had never felt anything quite like it. His blood roared in his veins, his heart pounded, his breath stuttered. Then Denny was moving again, his nose and tongue under Richard's balls, shifting away again before Richard could get used to the sensation or process it.

Denny lapped at the curve of Richard's hipbone. A continuous running motion over, around, into his navel, pressure, warmth, wet. Then it was gone. Working up, slowly and thoroughly, covering muscle and skin. Up to a nipple, catching it with sharp teeth until Richard had no option but to cry out, head thrust back, neck stretched tight and inviting.

But Denny shifted again, sucking on Richard's fingers, tongue pushing in between, hot breath on his wrist and arm, in the crook of an elbow. Teeth pulled at the hair under Richard's arm and Richard's breath faltered, stuck in his chest. Such an intimate gesture. It shouldn't have been so hot, shouldn't have made Richard's muscles quiver and tense.

But then it was suddenly gone as Denny traveled on, nipping at Richard's shoulder, the base of his throat, pressing against the flesh of his neck, making Richard feel vulnerable and small. Hands in his hair, controlling, holding him. Warm breath on his eyes, his ears, making his skin tingle and vibrate.

"Eyes closed." Denny huffed against his temple before tracing the outline of his lips with a deliberate tongue.

Richard fought to comply. The touch of Denny's breath felt physical against his skin. Then Denny's tongue was in his mouth, driving deep, deeper than anyone had ever been before. The weight and feel of his body, hard against Richard's, covered him, controlling, pressing into the bones of his hip.

Denny's breath, Denny's tongue, his mouth, his hands with their license to roam freely wherever they liked, his firm body, the power beneath the skin. Mouth taken and used. Legs pinning him down, sharp bones against his, hard cock pressing over and over and over into his side, thrusting. Hands cupping, gripping, tense and hard.

A warm splash on his skin and again. A groan near his ear.

Forehead resting against his, breath panting on his cheek.

Richard turned and twisted, pleading, trying to find that mouth, that tongue again.

"Hold still, it's coming," Denny gasped, voice warm and ragged. "Keep 'em closed."

He dropped kisses onto Richard's eyelids, then he was gone and Richard felt lost. But no. Firm hands over his skin, tracing a pattern down, down, down. Hot, wet lips on his cock. Pressure and friction and Richard was curving up from the bed, spine bowed right over as he came and came into Denny's mouth and onto his face.

Then... Then the weight of the world, all it was and all he'd lost, came crowding in, fogging Richard's brain, blinding him. He twisted his arms across himself, binding himself. He couldn't stop shaking, tremors that wound the length of his body.

Then Denny's arms were around him, holding him tight enough to burst. Tight enough to lean against, to let himself go. Denny around him, over him, surrounding him. Holding him in.

If these were Richard's issues with touching, he knew they were going to take a hell of a time to crack.

Chapter Four

It took Denny another eight days to crack under the boredom. At first it was subtle, a meal cooked when Richard got back, a door that no longer stuck, a cupboard fixed, a pile of trash outside cleared. Then he was asking for jobs. Did Richard want the room painted? The old outbuilding fixed? The roof tiles put back?

Richard smiled and said yes to whatever Denny wanted.

Eight days in which Denny explored the house and the grounds outside searching for clues about Richard's past, then investigated the local area. He bought things with a credit card that had his name on it, something that still made him stop and think. Days in which he wandered around trying to decide what he actually wanted to do, what he actually liked. He'd never had the choice before, never really thought about it.

Some days he'd go out with his wrist deliberately uncovered, the red patch of healing scar tissue clearly visible, waiting for, almost daring, someone to react.

But they didn't. They just looked at it, then him, before putting his purchases in a bag. Other days he'd keep it covered and wonder at the anonymity it brought. Slaves had never been common. Everybody knew about them but not many had them. They were simply too expensive. Those that did exist were mostly kept safely under lock and key.

Without his brands, Denny found people hardly noticed him.

Eight days of getting used to the new order, of trying to work out what he wanted, what he felt. Who he was.

Eight days of working on Richard's issues with touching.

Night after night he pushed Richard, trying to take him beyond his comfort zone, to get him to reciprocate the amazing night of touching and response. But when Richard tried, Denny could feel waves of self-consciousness and embarrassment coming off him. Mostly Richard ended up laughing loudly before, pushing Denny down and blowing him instead. But Denny knew that was an easy escape route for him. If Denny made him try too hard Richard would get up from the bed, face closed tight, and walk away.

But what had also come as a surprise to Denny was how much he liked to touch. He'd started doing it just to get Richard used to it. A hand to his back, pressure on his arm or elbow, a thigh or shoulder pressed against his when they sat on the sofa watching TV. It had shocked Denny just how much he liked contact with another person. He hadn't had that in so long and he knew Richard didn't want anything from him. It didn't mean anything except contact. At first Richard had looked at him sideways then he shrugged and started to lean in when Denny pressed.

But Denny suspected that kind of touching had been normal between Richard and Grady.

They went out to the bar on a few nights and Denny slowly learned to relax around the others until they became just regular people, not faces he knew from the newspapers. A couple of times Harley had turned up at the house or come back with Richard, often late at night. A bottle of whiskey had been passed around and Denny had learned to relax with him as well. Usually they got drunk, laughing about things that had happened or Harley doing wicked impressions of people that had Denny feeling faintly guilty for finding it so funny. Sometimes the talk turned serious, about current problems or mistakes from the past.

One time Harley had stopped midsentence, looked at Denny, and said, "Sorry." Short and curt.

Denny had mumbled a reply, not knowing how to respond.

And if Harley still called him Tassel Boy? Hell, so what? Denny liked that jacket. That was one thing he was sure about.

Those nights mostly ended with them all passing out on the sofa, chairs, and bed. But before Harley left he always rested a hand on the back of Richard's neck and said, "I hope you know what you're doing."

Denny remembered thinking the same thing himself, back at the start.

* * * *

Richard admired the enormous steak in front of him. Denny could cook, he'd give him that, and this one was done to perfection. It was just he couldn't ever remember eating this much red meat before. There'd never been the money. And after Grady died? He'd never cared enough to cook.

To savor it slowly or dig right in? Dig in, it was the only way.

"Are you not eating?" He looked over at Denny, who was playing with his food.

"Yeah." Denny nodded distractedly. "I can't quite get my head around the fact I'm about to say this, but I'm bored."

"I wondered how long it would take you to crack. To be honest, I'm surprised you lasted this long," Richard said around a mouthful of food. Heaven on his taste buds.

"So what do I do?"

"I don't know. What do you want to do?"

"I have no idea," Denny admitted. "Never had the choice, never thought about it, never…"

"Think about it now. Nothing is set in stone and you can change your mind whenever you like. But what do you enjoy doing? Is it something you could make a life out of?"

Denny shrugged, chewing at his lip as he lined up his food in a neat pattern. "I like cooking. I'm quite good at that."

"Do you want to go to cooking school? We could find out about it."

"That's the trouble, I don't know. Would I enjoy doing it properly or do I just like making dinner when I'm in the mood?" He suddenly smiled, more like his normal self. "This fucking freedom stuff is hard. It comes with decisions and it isn't as easy as you think."

"Nothing ever is," Richard agreed. "What do you want to do?"

"Can I get a job? In a restaurant or diner? Somewhere small and grimy where it won't matter if I make mistakes. Then I can see if I like it."

Richard fought back the answer that Denny already had a job. "You don't have to ask my permission," he said instead. "That comes with freedom as well. But you don't have to get a job."

"I know that. But will you help me find one? I haven't got a clue where to start."

"That I can do." Richard nodded. "I'll ask around. Somebody will know somebody who's hiring." He looked back at his food—it really was an awesome steak but already half gone—and thought about who to contact. It wouldn't take more than a quick phone call, two at the most. There were an awful lot of people just about bursting to do him a favor. Nearly as many as those that'd like to burn him alive.

"Richard?"

"Hmm?" There was a guy who owned a diner the other side of town that would help. No, too far away if Denny didn't have the car.

"You and Grady ever fuck?"

"What?" Richard stopped, forkful of meat halfway to his mouth.

"Did you and Grady ever fuck? You know, up the ass stuff."

"I know what fucking is." Richard forced his mouth closed. "What the hell brought that question on?"

"Well, we're going around in circles with your touching issues and—"

"I don't have touching issues," Richard interrupted.

"Sure you do," Denny said matter-of-factly. "I thought it was time we stuck that on the back burner for a while and moved on to something else. So back to my question. Did you two ever fuck?"

"I…" Sometimes Richard felt like he was being railroaded by Denny and his logic. Denny tilted his head and waited for an answer. "I never fucked him. There was no way he was going to…"

"I figured as much from what you said. Have to admit I never realized he'd been that badly hurt. You wouldn't have known from the newspapers or seeing him on the TV."

"He didn't want to look like a victim or a martyr," Richard said as he thought back to another time.

"Even though that's what he ended up becoming." Denny knew how much Grady's death had affected events. "So." He brought the subject back around. "You've never fucked anyone. Did he fuck you?"

"A few times." Richard's cheeks started to heat up. Why the hell should he be embarrassed about saying this? He'd already told Denny his secrets. "I knew he didn't really want to do it. He couldn't stand the idea of hurting me. But I didn't mind, I wanted it. I loved that connection with him, the feel of him inside me. I needed it. I could put up with anything for that."

"Whoa, wait a minute." Denny stopped him. "You saying it hurt?"

"Well, yeah."

"Always?"

"Yeah, sort of. But not much and I didn't care because—"

"Richard." Denny stopped him again. "It doesn't have to hurt. Maybe a bit uncomfortable at first but it doesn't always have to hurt."

"Come on, I've heard what guys say. But we all know that's just a bit of bravado or they're into weird shit. I'm not like that."

"It doesn't have to hurt," Denny said again.

Richard stared at him, unsure. "I've had your cock in my mouth. I know just how big it is. There's no way that goes up anyone's ass without you knowing about it."

"Oh, you'll know about it, all right." Denny stared at him. "You're supposed to know about it. But if I work you right, work you up and open, you aren't going to be hurting."

Richard felt like the last piece of steak was stuck halfway down his throat, like he'd forgotten how to swallow.

"You want it? You want to try another lesson?" Denny had given up any pretense of eating. "You want to try fucking? I don't care if you fuck me or I do you. I like it either way."

"Me fuck you?"

"Is that what you want to do?"

"I... I don't know how..."

"Sure you do. You know how to fuck. It's hardwired into every man. You want to fuck me or do you want me to show you how to make it good first?"

"I don't know." The words came out as almost as a whisper.

"With freedom come decisions. That's what you told me, and I trust you." Denny stared at him, eyes sharp and steady. "Do you trust me when I say I'll make it good?"

Richard's throat felt dry and raspy, the very air dragging on it. "Yes."

"Then I'm telling you it's time we fucked. Now you tell me which way around."

"You...you fuck me. Show me how."

"Okay." Denny pushed his chair back from the table, long legs spread wide, his hard cock pressing visibly against the confines of his jeans. "Come on then."

"What? Now?" Richard all but squeaked.

"Yes, now. What's there to wait for?" Denny flicked the button free, letting the zip pull open as he got up, heading for the bedroom.

Richard exhaled very slowly before pushing himself up. He was just about to follow when he made for the cupboard instead. Finding the whiskey, he took a long swallow straight from the bottle then one more. He needed more than luck right now.

Denny had pulled the covers back and was lying stretched out on the mattress, completely naked. "Come on," he said softly, and all of a sudden Richard knew he did trust him. If he was going to learn, this was the only person he trusted enough to teach him.

He slipped out of his clothes quickly and climbed onto the bed. "If I do something wrong, just say so and I'll—"

Denny reached up and caught him around the back of the neck, pulling him down until he was pressed over Denny.

"Shut up, man." Denny grinned before kissing him hard, fucking his tongue deep into his mouth. "Shut up and relax."

Richard let his eyes fall shut as he rode the pleasure.

Denny kept kissing him, holding Richard's face, cupping his cheek, pressing his fingers into Richard's flesh in a way that made his skin heat up under the touch. His other hand seemed to be everywhere, skimming over his shoulder blades, stroking down Richard's spine, rubbing at his hip. Somehow Denny managed to push a leg between his, hooking Richard's knee upward, then there was a hand smoothing over Richard's ass, gliding into the gap.

Richard would have dearly loved to stop the breathy little gasp, but it was out before he had any idea it was even there. He knew Denny heard it.

On and on Denny kissed, taking control and possession of Richard's mouth, one hand in his hair, touching his eyelids, stroking across his shoulders and back as the other ghosted over his ass. Richard shoved his clenched fists into Denny's shoulders, worry gnawing at him that it was the wrong act. He should move his hands, should be touching Denny as well. He didn't know what he should do.

Then Denny's tongue was deeper in his mouth, fucking and filling, Richard couldn't think anymore, didn't want to.

Next thing Richard knew, he was being rolled over onto his back and pushed into the pillow, even though Denny's tongue never left his mouth. His legs were eased apart and it felt like the most natural thing in the world for Denny to be in between them. Denny's hands still moved over his body in a way that wouldn't let Richard think, wouldn't let him focus or concentrate.

A wet, firm finger, not going in him, just on him, testing the muscle, letting him feel the promise. And when had Denny got lube? Where had he hidden it? And was Richard really going to fight to think about it or was he just going to trust?

Denny sucked on his tongue, thumb rubbing at the head of Richard's cock, and Richard forgot what the question was.

More pressure against him, more slick and glide, and Richard pressed his hips down toward it. "Whoa, slow down, tiger, not yet," Denny said into his mouth. "Not for a long time. I want you ready and me desperate for it."

"But I—"

"Shh." Denny rose up onto his knees, still licking across Richard's lips. "Trust your good old buddy, I know what I want."

Richard again felt himself being rolled, this time onto his belly. He wasn't sure about that, he couldn't reach Denny's mouth this way. At least he knew what to do with his hands now, balling them up under his face but...he liked Denny's mouth. He knew about kissing and oh...Denny's lips were on his neck, between his shoulder blades, sucking and licking. Denny reached down between his cheeks and Richard was spreading his legs again before he knew what he was doing.

The wet slick pressure of a finger circling over and over, on and on, until Richard was sweating, desperate to push toward it. It was too much. Too intense, too much feeling. He couldn't let himself go. Couldn't. Then there was a little push into his body, just testing the way, twisting and slip-sliding and Richard stilled. He swallowed deliberately and took back control, holding himself in that familiar, contained manner.

"No," Denny whispered the word. "Don't do that. Just relax and enjoy this as much as I am."

Then Richard felt one finger push in, easing its way as though there was no rush in the world. Two, as Denny lapped at his neck, nipped at his lips. Three, and Denny was whispering again, breath hot and damp on Richard's skin.

"That's it, relax just like that. Can you feel your muscle give and relax, welcoming my fingers inside? Now you need to let go completely, come on."

Another push in and Richard couldn't help his startled whimper of response, but still he kept his body tightly controlled. Again and Denny licked the sweat from his spine, down to the small of his back. Again and Richard's breath was coming in short, breathy gasps. Denny ran his tongue lower, following the line of his hand, circling his fingers, and Richard tensed even further.

"Let me," Denny insisted. "I know you don't...but, just fucking let me. Don't you get it? I want it, need it, so screw your fucking self-control and let me."

Richard had never been pushed this hard before. He went still under Denny. "Go on, do it."

Denny huffed. "Not what I wanted but I'll take what I can get."

Denny slid his tongue forward, slipping around his fingers, pressing in between, breath hot, saliva running down into the mix. He pulled his fingers out, pushing his tongue in and groaned. He fucked into Richard's body the same way he'd fucked into his mouth, over and over, long and slow as his hands gripped and pulled at flesh.

Richard lay motionless and took it all, panting hard.

Without warning, Denny plunged his fingers back in, sliding them deeper, farther, pressing right where they should, making sure Richard's body had no choice but to respond. Yet Richard held himself tight.

"Fuck it, you can move. You can let me know if I'm doing something right. Move, make a noise, give me some sort of reaction."

"You are...it is...it's good," Richard said in a shaky voice. "I'm sorry if I'm not—"

"I've heard your sorrys before," Denny said. Then he was up and off and flipping Richard onto his back before Richard knew it was happening. "Just fucking relax, would you?" He spread Richard's legs wider still and pushed his way between them, lifting his knees up. "Just close your eyes and think of porn or anything you like that turns you on."

Only Richard didn't want to think about anything other than the heat in his ass as Denny slid two fingers back in and—oh shit—the wet sucking friction on his dick.

It was like Richard's entire world was focused on those few square inches of flesh between his cock and his ass as Denny timed his movements to perfection, sucking and fucking with his fingers. It was a faultless rhythm with no gaps for Richard to catch his breath or think about anything other than just lying there—perfect pleasure that went around in circles and was in danger of short-circuiting his brain. He pulled his head back, stretching his neck and staring up at the ceiling, waiting for the world to explode.

"Is that it?" Denny said, not unkindly, more resigned. "Is that all you're capable of?"

Richard wasn't moving, wasn't reacting, even though he knew it would be obvious to the whole world that he was enjoying himself. Maybe that really was it, he thought. Maybe that was all he was capable of.

But Denny didn't give him a chance to think any further. Instead he sat up and hooked Richard's legs around his arms as he leaned over him, hands on the mattress at either side of Richard's waist.

"It would be easier if you were on your belly, but I want to see your face." Denny breathed on Richard's knee when he slid carefully inside in one long, smooth glide. His own breath caught for a moment.

Then Denny eased almost all the way out again before pressing back home, smooth and decisive. Richard's eyes opened wider and wider, his mouth frozen in an O shape.

"Jesus fuck, am I hurting you?" Denny asked. "After all the promises I've made, are you all right?"

"Oh, God, yes," Richard panted. "Do it again, now."

Denny did, pulling back easy, then a slow but firm push back in. Richard's back arched off the bed, a muffled curse escaping his mouth as he flailed his hand around until it caught onto Denny's arm in a tight grip, the other going up to his head. "Again." Richard was demanding now.

"This?" Denny grinned down at him. "This is what it takes to break through your ingrained control?" He bit at Richard's knee and began fucking with deliberate, methodical thrusts until Richard thought he might just burst.

Richard heaved against the sheets, twisting and tugging at Denny. He reached up, winding his hand in Denny's hair, and dragged him forward while he scrabbled and scratched at any bit of flesh he could reach. Richard knew he was coming apart in a way he'd never thought possible. This was making him break.

What it took to crack Richard was being fucked, sweetly and thoroughly.

Denny reached down and fisted Richard's cock. One, two quick pulls was all it took and Richard was shouting at the ceiling, hot liquid spilling between them. That seemed to be the trigger that tipped Denny over, making him thrust once more, hard and fast, before he too was coming.

He collapsed on top of Richard, face buried in his neck as he tried to catch his breath. Easing out carefully, he then rolled over, landing on his back, still puffing like a steam train. "Well, that lesson went well, don't you think?" He laughed, rubbing his hand over his face.

Richard stayed silent next to him. "It did, didn't it? It went well in the end?"

"I didn't know it could be like that," Richard said in a voice full of wonder and regret. "I thought I at least knew what I was missing, not that I minded. Turns out I was wrong, even on that."

"Are you okay?" Denny looked over at him.

"Yeah, I'm fine." He shook his head, a small, ironic gesture. "I might be a bit sore in the morning but right now I'm really fine, and isn't that just funny."

"How's it funny? Because of Grady?"

"He used to be really tentative because he was worried about hurting me, and he was right, he was. I'd try and pretend he wasn't but..." He dragged in a breath, eyes fixed on the ceiling. "Neither of us knew it could be better."

"Hey, it was no one's fault if you didn't know. Don't beat yourself up now with what might have been." Denny reached out as though he were about to offer a comforting hand. But Richard looked at him and Denny hesitated before letting it fall.

"No, that's one thing I don't have to worry about. It couldn't have been any better." Richard fought to understand his feelings, to understand what had just happened.

"Why not?"

"Grady didn't really want sex of any kind. He'd have been quite happy never to have it. My dad sure fucked up more than just Grady's life." He turned to look at Denny, trying to stop all his emotions showing on his face. He wasn't convinced he was successful. "How about living with that? Knowing the man you love is doing something he doesn't want to, just for your sake. Oh, he'd pretend, but we both knew deep down."

"That must have been hard," Denny said tentatively. "On you both."

"Fuck, I didn't know a damned thing." Richard rubbed a hand over his face. "I thought all the panting and begging in porn films was fake. Can you imagine if I'd gone into a relationship with Simms like that? I'd have let him hurt me, would have thought it was normal. I wouldn't have known how to touch him or be touched or…" He pulled away, unwilling to let Denny see his face anymore, and sat on the edge of the bed with his back to Denny. "Thank you," he said formally, his voice tight. "Thank you for not letting me make a total fool of myself and leaving myself completely vulnerable and exposed."

Denny slid closer. "I'm officially adding 'thank you' to 'sorry' on the list of things I'll kick your ass for if you say them again. I have a hell of a lot more to thank you for."

"Maybe," Richard managed as his shoulders rounded and his head drooped forward.

Denny pressed against his side, running a hand softly over his back, across the scars. Richard didn't tense or pull away and, eventually, he even leaned in.

* * * *

Ten days later, Richard was in the shower when Denny came home from a shift at the job Richard had found for him. It wasn't the greatest job in the world, Richard thought, but the small diner near the house was exactly what Denny had asked for. Somewhere to learn, somewhere to find out if cooking was what he wanted to do.

The only trouble was, as soon as the job started, Richard had needed to go away on more freedom movement business. He'd been gone for just under a week after rumors had come in about a small rural community on the other side of the river. They'd been making life tough for released slaves, so he'd taken Harley and a few others and had gone to check things out.

But now he was back and waiting for Denny to get home.

He heard Denny banging around in the kitchen, then his name was called.

"In here," he yelled as he turned the shower off.

"Good trip?" Denny held out a towel when Richard opened the shower cubicle door. "Get everything done you wanted?"

"Yeah, in the end." Richard fixed the towel around his waist.

"You were gone longer than—what the hell happened?" Denny caught Richard's shoulder and pulled him away from the billowing steam where the scrapes and bruises on his chest were easier to see.

"Turns out they hadn't all released their slaves. A minority thought they could hang on to them. So we explained otherwise." Richard grinned, extremely pleased with himself.

"You got in a fight."

"A couple, actually, but you should see the other guys."

Denny turned him round, following the line of a deep scratch over Richard's bicep. "What the hell?" There were marks and cuts all over Richard's upper back, not deep or severe but enough to make you think.

"I fell over a fence. Well, maybe technically I got pushed, but definitely not thrown. No matter what Harley tells you," he said, pride thick in his voice.

"You could have been killed." Denny rubbed his thumb over each mark, seeming to ignore Richard's flinches.

"No way. We put three in the hospital. Two more needed sewing up or bones setting."

"Where else?" Denny pulled the towel away. There was a nasty black bruise over Richard's hip.

"Richard," Denny scolded.

"Shit, now I feel like I'm being told off. We got in a fight, it was fun. We won. It's no big deal and...fuck." He hissed as Denny's mouth came down over a scrape on his shoulder. Denny bit, none too lightly. "Oh..." The word stumbled out of his mouth seemingly of its own will.

"It was fun?" Denny licked along a cut and Richard arched back into it, unable to stop himself or his gasp.

"Sometimes...you know...it's kind of..." He tried to defend himself but Denny licked again.

"No, I don't know." Denny bit down hard at the juncture of neck and body, really hard, not letting go. Then he licked and lapped at the cuts and bruises.

"Yeah, it was kind of..." How was Richard supposed to remember what he was trying to say when...? Oh, dear God, Denny had his face pressed into skin, hands skimming Richard's hips as he crowded into his back.

"Shut up." Denny licked a smooth line over a particularly nasty scrape and Richard hissed again, pushing into it. Slowly Denny maneuvered him against the counter by the sink, forcing the way with body, chest and hands.

"But Harley and I, we like to let off steam and..."

Then Richard wasn't thinking about Harley at all when Denny mouthed at his wounds and large hands seemed to be everywhere on his body, holding him tight, taking control. Denny lifted his leg, rubbing something smooth and silky over and into Richard. Long slick fingers wrapped around his dick, squeezing him into full hardness, not letting him catch a breath in between strokes as he was pinned in place. Others sliding into him, easing him open, working him ruthlessly. "Shit," he gasped almost silently while it went on and on.

Hands, mouth, tongue like points of delicious pleasure until he couldn't hold his head up anymore. He let it fall back onto Denny's shoulder with heavy, hitching breaths.

Then all Richard could think about was Denny's cock. Think about it sliding into him, filling him deep, working him like it was taking possession of his body, hot and hard and concentrating all his attention. One of Denny's hands still worked his dick as the other splayed out across his chest, holding him flush against Denny. All Richard could think about was where Denny touched him. Flesh on flesh that tingled and burned, everything else forgotten.

Denny's thrusts were slow and calculated and suddenly Richard's breathing matched his, breath for thrust, his hips following along with the rhythm. Then Denny upped the pace, panting into Richard's neck, pulling him back to meet each and every stroke. Not only was Richard's breathing in time now, but so were his husky little gasps and the thump of his heart under Denny's hand. He reached back to grab onto Denny's hip and thigh, flexing his fingers in time with each thrust. All his control was gone in a rush of response that left him feeling open and exposed to Denny's hands and cock. To his eyes. Richard twisted and shivered under Denny, rocking with a lack of restraint that felt almost reckless.

Open. Control gone.

"Who knew?" Denny mouthed along Richard's stretched neck, over the bite mark he'd made as Richard twisted into the touch. "Who knew you could be this responsive." Richard simply let himself be held in place by Denny's body, giving himself over to it. "This, you just like this, this is what I want."

Then Denny altered the rhythm, pushing in and squeezing Richard's dick at the same time. Richard tensed, held still, his body not knowing which way to move, which sensation to follow. Again, and he was digging his fingers in hard, clutching at Denny, hanging on for dear life. Again, and it was all over as he came in long, shuddering pulses, his spine arching up, curving back.

But Denny wasn't finished yet. He caught hold of Richard's hips, fingers skimming over the dark bruise, mapping it, testing it, and thrust harder. When Richard started pushing back Denny stuttered, biting with desperate cries at his neck. He kept fucking until there was nothing left, until he started to go soft, and still he didn't stop. Little pushes and presses long after there was any point. Then Denny rested his forehead against Richard's shoulder, breathing hard, his arms curled around Richard tightly.

"Come on," Denny said eventually, his voice gone dry and raspy.

Next thing Richard knew he was being dragged to the bedroom and pushed onto his back. Denny flopped down next to him on his belly, jeans and boxers still at mid-thigh, his face pressed into the gap between Richard's arm and the mattress.

"Did you miss me then?" Richard asked with humor. "You've got used to all the sex."

"Nothing but my hand for over a week. What did you expect?"

Richard laughed, patting the back of Denny's head then leaving his hand there.

"Are you all right?" Denny asked. "I went a bit quick, maybe a bit hard? I haven't done that before."

"My shoulder hurts." Richard rubbed at the spot.

"Your shoulder?"

"You bit it. I've got teeth marks."

"And that hurts more than your ass?"

"No, my ass hurts way more, but that's kind of good. My shoulder's just sore."

Denny rolled over onto his side, looking up at Richard through his hair. "You want me to kiss it better?"

"My shoulder or my ass?"

"Both." Denny grinned.

"You're on, but later." Richard patted him again.

"You know, I'm thinking it's about time you put all this newfound knowledge into practice and fuck me."

"Now?" Richard's eyes rounded. "I'm not as young as I used to be."

"I'll give you a rain check, but not for long."

"Denny, you don't…" Richard started to argue. "I'm happy doing it this way. It's what I'm used to."

"Hey." It was Denny's turn to pat, high up on Richard's belly. "You've never fucked and every guy should fuck at least once. After, you can decide what you like best, but you should try it, unless you really hate the idea. You don't hate it, do you?"

"No, but…"

"Good, that's decided then. I'd be really disappointed if you didn't fuck me at all. So, next time." He traced a finger over the bruise on Richard's hip. "Look at the state of you. I let you out for one week and you come back like this."

"It's Harley's fault. He's a bad influence."

"You wait until I see him." He glanced up, his focus on Richard's face. "Any real damage?"

"No, only surface scratches." Richard relaxed, comfortable and easy.

"Good. Did the trip really go okay? Did you do good stuff?"

"Yeah, I honestly think we did. How about you, a good week? How's the job?"

"It's all right." Denny rolled onto his back, shoulder pressed against Richard's, jeans still around his thighs, soft cock resting on his groin. He made no move to adjust his clothes.

Richard looked at him for a long minute. "No it's not, is it? I can tell by your voice. You're not happy there."

"Yeah it is, it's fine and—"

"Shut up and tell the truth," Richard said gently.

"I guess it's not what I expected," Denny finally admitted. "I work harder there than I did as a slave. I thought it would be different, being free, but the others were never slaves and they're still treated like dirt half the time."

"Do you want to try somewhere else?"

"Maybe, yeah, I could—"

"Hey," Richard interrupted. "You don't have to. You don't have to work. You're rushing things. Stop and feel the wind on your face before you make any big decisions. This is all new to you and that place was only ever a stopgap."

"I have kind of decided I don't want to do that."

"What, work in a restaurant?"

"Yeah. I don't like people around me all the time. It gives me an itch in the middle of my back. I don't like being told what to do or when to do it. I don't like the buzz of so many people or the routine."

"So give up the job. I'll call them in the morning."

"Don't I have to work out a notice period or something?" Denny seemed to have already accepted quitting.

"Being Grady Porter's Richard has its advantages." Richard grinned. "Forget it and think about what else you might want to do."

"And what do I do while I'm thinking?"

"Watch daytime TV?"

"Fuck that, I'm not that desperate." Denny hitched up, wriggling against Richard. "There is something, though. Would you mind if I cleared the land around the house? Fixed things up, maybe grow some stuff?"

"Would I mind you getting this place back to how it should be?" Richard raised his eyebrows. "Like hell I would. You go for it, do whatever you want. What are you thinking, like a small holding or something?"

Denny shrugged. "I'm not sure, something like that. It's what I know. It's funny, I never realized it before, but I like working on the land, making something out of nothing."

"Plus you'd be your own boss. I'm sure not going to tell you what to do. Shit, I don't know anything."

"It'd be a chance to see if that's what I want. There're a lot of years ahead of me that daytime TV sure isn't going to fill."

"You go for it, man, if it makes you happy." Richard laid a hand on Denny's hip.

"And what are you going to do? Sit on your ass and watch me work?" Denny grinned.

"Are you going to get all sweaty?" Richard grinned back. "I kinda like your muscles and if they're going to be all sweaty..." He let the implication hang.

"Fuck off." Denny dismissed him with a laugh.

"Tell you what, you work and I'll play to stop you from getting bored. I brought my guitar back from Harley's."

"You can play the guitar?" Denny twisted around to look at Richard. "You never said."

"I'm not that good." Richard shrugged. "It's been over at Harley's for months."

"People used to play sometimes, at night, when there were other slaves around. It always fascinated me, how you could coax sounds like that from a piece of wood."

"Do you want me to teach you?" Richard asked, and it was Denny's turn to go slightly wide-eyed.

"Would you?"

"Sure, if you want." Richard suddenly realized how happy he was to do it. "Can I ask you something?" He rolled onto his side, slipping a hand under his face to prop himself up.

"Of course."

"How come...you just..." Richard stopped, unsure what his actual question was. "You accepted my deal really quickly. I didn't expect that. You're young, gorgeous, the world at your feet and I'd just told you that you were free. I didn't think you'd accept something like that without a lot of persuading."

Denny gave a non-committal shrug. "It wasn't that big a deal. A bit of sex for all you were offering seemed almost too good to be true."

"Grady wouldn't have seen it like that," Richard said very quietly.

"Grady got used really hard and nasty. I didn't."

"Even so, when you were still being held... You still didn't want it. It was still rape."

"You don't think like that, not when you're a slave. Having straightforward sex with someone is easy. You even get something out of it for yourself. That's not a big deal. It's more like working as a whore. What you don't want is to get hurt, whether that's during sex or just getting a bad beating. I'd have rather spread my legs for some guy who wasn't going to hurt me than take a fist to the guts or a whip across my back. I never got hurt during sex so it was never a big thing. From what you've said it was completely different for Grady. He did get hurt."

"He always got hurt," Richard admitted.

"I didn't and I learned how to use it to my advantage. Sex was easy."

"So taking my deal was easy?"

"You're Grady Porter's Richard. It sort of felt like I was doing my bit for the cause." Denny had the decency to smile at that. "You seemed lost. Helping you out was easy."

"Oh great." Richard shook his head, curling his lips gently. "So I was a pity fuck."

"Well, you weren't exactly a hardship. Have you looked in the mirror recently? You're fucking gorgeous, and with all the heartbreak in those eyes, it was the least I could do." Denny laughed loudly. "Hell, I might have paid you for it, if I'd had any money."

"You're a fucking bastard, you know that?" Richard pushed at Denny's shoulder, but it was only softly and he was still smiling. "But, you know, I am sorry, even now."

"For what?"

"I'm still forcing you to make that decision. You're still working, and like Harley said, it's not right."

Denny rolled around, looking straight at Richard, grin still in place. "Trust me, man. This is a job made in heaven. I get to teach you to do everything exactly the way I like it and I get sex whenever I want. Hell, I don't even have to feel guilty for not buying you flowers first. I just tell you it's time for another lesson and you're downright grateful. Does life get any better than that?"

Yeah, Richard thought, it did. But he wasn't quite sure how to explain it to Denny.

Chapter Five

Denny decided it was time to put the lesson on Richard fucking him into practice the following morning.

It didn't go quite as well as he'd hoped.

First Richard moaned about morning breath then got a fit of the giggles when he kneeled on Denny's hair and finished with a cramp in his calf muscle. Denny couldn't work out what Richard's knee was doing up near his hair but when Richard offered a mutual blow, he forgot all about knees and fucking. Instead he teased Richard for as long as possible, making Richard actually God-honest beg to be allowed to come, before enjoying a most satisfying orgasm then going to start work outside.

They used the rest of the day to work out what supplies would be needed and wandering around agricultural shops. The evening was spent bent close, shoulder to shoulder, over the guitar.

* * * *

Next evening, after a hard day clearing decades of crap from just one small corner of the land around the house, Denny decided it was time to try the lesson again.

Start off subtly. "Richard," he bellowed from the bed across to the bathroom. "Have you ever been up close and personal with an ass?"

"Nope," came the nonchalant, toothpaste-muffled reply.

In Denny's opinion, not a great beginning, but hell, everyone had to start somewhere.

Fifteen minutes later he was giving really helpful advice, only Richard didn't seem to agree.

"Would you just shut up, man?" Richard huffed, sitting back on his heels. "I get it, all right, I get it. It's not rocket science. I can work out which bit of me goes where inside you."

"I'm only trying to be helpful. Knowledge is power and all that." Denny lifted his leg a little higher, trying to hook it over Richard's shoulder.

"Next you'll be drawing me a fucking diagram."

"You think it'd help?"

Ten minutes after and things had got worse. At least Richard seemed to think so. "If you say another fucking word, so help me God, next time I go down on you I'll bite your dick off," he growled against Denny's calf.

A further handful of minutes and Denny really, really needed Richard to start listening to him. "When someone is grabbing at your ass, trying to drag you in, and yelling at you to 'just give it to me, big boy', trust me, they fucking mean it." He pulled at Richard's hair. "Stop being so fucking girly and do me already."

"You swear too much when—"

"Richard, get your fucking fingers out of my ass and get your dick in there."

Richard shrugged and did as he'd been told.

Then, much to Denny's surprise, the shouting, the constant arranging and rearranging of limbs, the moaning and the slip-sliding through too much lube were all forgotten when Richard gave a sigh of surprise and sank deep inside him.

Denny would swear he heard Richard mutter the word 'heaven' quietly. Then the next moment Richard seemed to have instinctively remembered the age-old rhythm of all men as he fucked deep and perfect. All Denny had to do was concentrate on the pleasure. Concentrate on that as he rested a hand gently on the back of Richard's neck and pleaded for 'more' and 'now'. Then he was whispering 'yes', and 'God' and Richard's name.

Richard looked down at him, his eyes blown wide. "I didn't know it could be like this. I didn't know."

Afterward Denny flopped out across the mattress, smiling smugly as he stroked Richard's belly.

"I didn't know it could be like that," Richard said again. "But now that I've actually tried it, I've decided I rather like fucking."

"That's my boy," Denny said and his smile grew even bigger.

* * * *

The bar on Friday night had been an excellent idea. They'd tried other places but Richard had never quite managed to relax, and after a few hours in a couple of different ones, Denny had agreed the movement's was easier to go to. At the others, sooner or later someone recognized Richard then the little nudges and sly glances started. Then the not so sly ones. People came over wanting autographs, to talk, to shake his hand, to demand he personally compensate them for the cost of the slaves their parent, husband, sister, friend had been made to release.

Even when things stayed quiet Richard sat, back ramrod straight, waiting for it to happen.

It was simply easier at their bar, discreet, secure, protected, friendly, plus the beer was cheap. Eventually Denny had learned to not only relax but to really enjoy the time he spent there. People had gotten used to him to the extent that no one felt obliged to talk to him anymore if Richard was off someplace else. Richard seemed to earn that kind of care from his friends. These people supported him without his even asking.

When the couple Denny had been talking to at the bar got deep into an argument that dredged up things that had happened over ten years ago, he smiled and figured it was time to leave them to it and head back to his table. A couple had to have been together a long time for arguments like those.

He tipped the chair back on its hind legs, swirled his beer, and watched Richard.

So, Richard could fuck. That morning's immensely anticipated repeat performance had proved that just fine. Denny adjusted himself on the seat, pressing down against the chair. Yep, Richard fucked damned, damned fine. A grin curled at his lips as the ache curled in his ass.

He started to consider Richard as he moved from one group to another. Denny was sure he looked different lately, less tense. Less like he had a rod up his ass. His shoulders weren't always hunched and he enjoyed himself more, laughing with people when before he would have just stood and watched. Maybe all he had needed were rods and asses—or cocks, if you were being more literal—to make him less on edge. Funny to think that's what it had taken to break his self-control and make him relax. To turn Richard into the quietly, wonderfully, responsive guy Denny was starting to get to know. Whatever, he looked good for it. Richard had always been a handsome man, now he was...better.

People stopped when Richard came their way, their faces turned toward him. This place was pretty egalitarian but at first Denny had thought there was a definite hierarchy. The more senior the leader, the more deference they got. It had taken him a while to realize it wasn't like that. Admiration came not from position or appearance, but from respect, and that had to be earned.

Detlef Meyer was the top of the pile whichever way you thought about it, but Richard? Richard was quietly, discreetly respected. Fuck knew why, it had nothing to do with him after all, but Denny was proud of him for that.

"What're you grinning like a runaway from a mental home for, Tassel Boy?" Harley slid into the chair next to Denny and yawned expansively.

"Nothing." Denny swung on the legs of his chair. "Would you quit with the 'Tassel Boy'? This is an awesome jacket." He pulled at a couple of the trimmings. He'd lost some along the way but he thought it looked better because of it, more worn and lived in.

"It's all right." Harley shrugged. "I had one like it when I was about twelve. Whatever, if you have the guts to wear it, then you go for it."

Denny swigged his beer and thought about that, insult or compliment? He had no idea.

"You're watching Richard," Harley commented, a long pause later.

"Yeah, I was just thinking he seems more relaxed than I've seen him before. He looks good for it."

Again Harley was silent for a while as he seemed to quietly assess Denny. Before he spoke his gaze went to Richard, watching him on the other side of the room. "Denny." There was no humor in his voice, no lightness. This was serious. "You know I keep saying I hope he knows what he's doing. Well, I hope you do too."

"Are you threatening me again?" Denny asked. "You don't have to, I get it. You'll kill me if I hurt him."

Harley nodded, just once, short and swift. "I will but...if you're just trying to milk as much as you can get from him, then don't. You want money, you come to me."

"You want to pay me to have sex with you as well?" Denny raised an eyebrow. "Sorry, but I've got an exclusive deal going."

"That's not what I mean." Harley glanced at Richard again. "He'll play fair by you, paying you whatever you agreed. You've got no worries on that."

"I'm not worried," Denny said.

"But don't push him, don't try for more. If you do then you and me will have a problem." He turned toward Denny, his eyes hard. "If that's your game, if you see Richard as some kind of meal ticket, then you'd better talk to me now. I'll pay you to fuck off, right this second. I'll pay you a hell of a lot and I won't even break your legs before I do it. If you've got any kind of game plan or angle, I'm advising you to take my offer and go."

Denny felt pinned fast under Harley's gaze, even though every muscle was screaming at him to run and his heart was hammering in his chest. Run and hide, somewhere safe, somewhere a long, long way away from this menacing, deeply intimidating man. He licked at his lips, mouth suddenly bone dry. "I don't know what you think I am but..."

"That's the whole point. I'm having trouble trusting my gut instinct." Harley shook his head, face scrunching up. "I've got good at sizing up people real quick. But you, this? This is too important for me to fuck up on. So I'm offering you a way out now."

Denny's gaze was drawn to Richard. Richard, who was laughing and smiling and...relaxed. Pushing the air from his lungs, he forced himself to look at Harley straight on. "I know Richard will play fair by me and I'll do the same by him. I'll do what he expects me to, what he's paying me to, and I'm not after more. For what it's worth, you have my word on that. He's too good a man to do otherwise."

For the longest while Harley sat, his attention fixed on Denny, then he nodded, face relaxing. "You want to play pool? I'm fucking useless at it but I'm always good for a laugh."

No extra threat needed.

* * * *

It took Denny long enough but with weeks of work he managed to clear the land, turn over the soil and plant his first crops. Now his back hurt like a bitch. A few days off—apart from a bit of watering—were what he needed now. Only that meant daytime soaps on TV. Fuck, he could do without them.

He lay in the bath, knees bent to accommodate his legs, beer in one hand, candy in the other, and wished Richard would get back so he could turn the radio up. Not fair if he had to get out and do it himself.

The door slammed as Richard came in and Denny waited for the slap of the fridge door and the pop of the beer cap before he called out.

"You got a lot done today." Richard leaned against the doorframe. "It looks good out there."

"I'm paying for it now. Everything aches." Denny stretched, causing the water to slosh close to the edge. "I've gone soft since I came down from the mountains."

"I wouldn't exactly call you soft." Richard's eyes darkened. "But take it easy for a while, there's no rush."

"We could have a day in tomorrow." Denny looked up through his wet hair. "Spend the whole time in bed. What do you say?"

"I'd love to." Richard licked at his lips. "But I can't. Harley and I have got a job in the next town over. There's some problem between former owners and ex-slaves. It shouldn't be hard to sort out but it needs doing."

"Shit, I don't want to stay here on my own. I get bored."

"Go into town, do some shopping, watch a movie or something."

"No, boring without you around. Hey." He suddenly sat up. "Can I come with you?"

"What, with me and Harley? I..." Richard appeared to think about it. "I don't see why not, as long as you stick close and keep out of trouble."

"Excellent. Now how about you take me to bed and make me forget all about my aching back?"

"Now that's an offer I have no intention of turning down." Richard grinned, already undoing his belt.

* * * *

The journey out took a few hours so they left nice and early. Richard drove Harley's 4x4 while Harley rode shotgun and Denny sprawled out in the back seat, watching the changing view. He'd never been this way before, never seen the new high-rise housing developments on the edge of town or the immaculately manicured golf courses. It all seemed alien and, to be honest, not particularly interesting.

When they arrived, Harley and Richard were greeted like visiting royalty by some, with marked hostility by others, but with respect by all—even if that respect was given grudgingly at times. They shook hands, slapped backs, listened carefully, and offered advice and reassurances. They acknowledged the grievances people felt but challenged their resentment and aggression. They negotiated, talked people down, and took a stand when needed, all while doing their damnedest to keep everyone on their side and feeling respected. Hours and hours of work to make sure the ex-slaves were protected and their position secure. Hours and hours of work to make sure everyone knew there was no going back.

Denny watched it all, fascinated. Harley was his normal confident presence, making people stop and take a step back as he passed. Richard was different. Gone was any of the hesitancy, uncertainty, or even the unrestrained passion Denny sometimes saw in bed. This man was self-assured, animated, forceful and very much in control. He knew how to get things done and he meant to do it.

They settled things, not to everyone's satisfaction, but they made sure everyone knew the new laws and were following them. Then they spent time chatting without rushing anyone. That was also part of the service. Denny had to admit he was impressed with both of them, the job they did and how they worked together. If Richard was an ambassador and enforcer for the freedom movement, then he was a hard-working and fucking good one.

It was early evening by the time they headed back to the car. It had been left at the side of the town's courthouse so they'd had a chance for a quick look around before meeting the concerned parties. Now they were regretting the distance, simply wanting to get home.

"You drive," Richard said to Harley. "All that talking's worn me out."

"I did just as much. I'm just as tired," Harley hit back.

"Yeah, but I drove up here."

"So?"

"You drive." Richard threw the keys at Denny. "In fact, next time you can drive both ways and we can sleep." He grinned.

"There's going to be a next time?" Denny asked.

"Sure, I don't see why not. Unless you were really bored. Even then I don't see why you shouldn't suffer like the rest of us and—Harley." The last word was spat out, low and full of intent.

Immediately Harley tensed, obviously attuned to everything around him, assessing the situation.

It took Denny a few seconds longer to realize what was going on. Richard had indicated a small group of men lying in wait for them. Some they'd been talking to just a few hours before. A couple had knives in their hands. All had trouble in their eyes.

"Not again." Harley huffed, sounding more resigned than anything else. "All I want is a nice cold beer but I guess we have to do this first. Ready, Ritchie?"

"Yeah." Richard circled around closer to Harley. "Denny, go get in the car. They don't have a problem with you."

"No time for that," Harley said as the first men moved out of the shadows. "Stay close, Tassel Boy."

"I can take care of myself and help," Denny argued. "I'm not exactly useless or small."

"Leave it to us. We know what we're doing." That was definitely an order from Harley.

Richard glanced over briefly and Denny couldn't work out what the fierce brightness in his eyes meant.

"Stay real close to me," Richard said, voice tight.

Then things turned almost surreal.

Denny thought it was like something from the movies, a fight scene that had been choreographed down to the last move, only he knew it wasn't. Harley and Richard fought with ease and confidence, anticipating each other's moves, covering each other's backs, knowing what to do and following commands given with a single word or a silent look. Their skill was obvious in every stance they took, every lean and economical line of attack. They knew what they were doing as improvised weapons were thrown between them with scarcely a glance.

Denny didn't join in, knowing he'd only interfere with an evidently well-oiled machine. Didn't interfere until another man, holding a long, thin-bladed knife, slipped out of hiding and headed toward Richard's flank. Then he didn't think. All sensible reasoning was forgotten as he rushed forward in a blur of movement and crashed into the man's back, pushing him off-balance. But it didn't last long. In a split second the man turned and the knife was being brought up toward Denny's belly.

It was Harley that stopped him. Stopped him with a vicious kick to the back of his knee and a twist of the guy's wrist that was accompanied by the sound of bones breaking. Harley stopped him while Denny was still working out what was happening. Next thing he knew the man was on the ground at his feet, blood pouring from a slash across his face. The knife was now in Richard's hand and the rest of the men were already disappearing back into nothingness.

Denny simply stood, fixed in place, and stared until a hand suddenly grabbed at the back of his neck, pulling his hair hard.

"Move," Richard said, his face white and tight, looking like barely controlled thunder. "In the car. Now." And he was practically thrown into the back.

Richard climbed in the driver's seat, all arguments about whose turn it was to drive forgotten, and in the next moment the engine was gunned and they were off and up the road. Harley made a quick call on his cell phone, reporting in what had happened. "They'll be dealt with," he said to Richard.

Then there was silence except for the sound of harsh breathing.

No more than ten minutes later Richard pulled the car off the road at the edge of town, near some old abandoned buildings. He stopped hard, tires crunching on the gravel, and was out the door and dragging Denny by his collar again before Denny even had time to think.

"Richard?" Denny asked.

"Move," came the demand as he was pulled sharply across the open space and slammed up against the wall.

"But..."

Denny vaguely heard Harley calling Richard's name, but Richard didn't even acknowledge it.

"He was going to kill you." Richard pushed hard, palm against Denny's chest, pinning him to the wall. "I told you to stay close, to keep out of trouble."

"I thought that—"

"Don't think. That way you die. Just do as you're fucking told." Richard shoved in closer, chest firm against Denny's.

Then his tongue was deep in Denny's mouth, not thrusting, not moving, just reaching in, possessing. Denny opened wider and let him. In the next moment, a button was flicked and Richard pushed a hand down the front of Denny's jeans. Then Denny was squeezed and pulled into hardness and on through to desperation in a matter of moments. Denny gasped, hanging between Richard and the wall. One minute his blood was pumping with adrenaline, the next his hips were hitching and flexing against Richard's hand as his orgasm was dragged from him.

Richard was already turning away and wiping his hand down the thigh of his jeans as Denny caught his breath. "Get back in the car," Richard ordered, striding over to it.

Denny looked up to see Harley still leaning on the hood, standing guard. "You might want to put that back in your pants before you do." Harley nodded toward Denny's exposed cock. He smiled, a small gift of support, then his gaze was gone. "Richard, are you—" Harley tried to ask as Richard snatched open the door.

"Shut up," Richard snapped. "I'm driving."

The rest of the drive back was again made in silence, the atmosphere charged.

Harley tried to reason again when he dropped them off at the house, getting out to take Richard's vacated seat. "Go easy, Ritchie. Talk to me if—"

"Not now," Richard cut him off, pulling and pushing at Denny once more.

"But—"

"No." With that, Richard kicked the front door shut behind him.

"Look, I'm sorry if I—" Denny tried, but Richard wasn't listening to him either.

"You shut up as well," Richard said, his voice clipped and tight. He pushed Denny through to the bedroom, stripped him efficiently, then fucked him through the mattress, fast and deadly thorough.

Denny fell asleep with one of Richard's hands splayed out over his belly, the other tangled deep in his hair, holding on way too tight.

* * * *

When Denny woke the following morning, Richard's side of the bed was still warm but empty. He stretched, feeling every ache in his body, glorying in how he got each and every one, before pulling on some clothes and going to find Richard.

He was sitting on the back step, empty coffee mug between his feet, watching the sun warm the land. He nodded a greeting, scooting over to make room for Denny. "You okay?" Richard asked. "After yesterday?"

"Yeah," Denny said, shuffling his naked feet on the ground. "You sure know how to fight." Denny started with what was easy.

"Yeah."

"I mean, you really know how to fight." It was more an impressed observation than anything.

"Of course I do," Richard said, his voice level. "We all had to learn. Made sure we had real lessons."

There was a long pause while Denny thought about that, then he asked abruptly, "Have you ever killed anyone?"

"Denny," Richard said, nose wrinkling and eyes squinting as he stared off into nowhere. "It was never a walk in the park. When things got serious they just wanted us dead, sent everything they could after us. Later, as they got more desperate, it got worse and we expected trouble all the time. If we didn't learn to fight we died. It really was as simple as that."

"I never thought about it," Denny admitted. "Never thought about how much hate there was toward the freedom movement. I don't know. I guess I just thought everyone must have seen how right you were once you explained it."

"There's still a lot of hate now. We took away their privileges. Of course they hate us."

Denny let out a long, slow breath. "It's my turn to thank you then. You and Harley and all the others who made it possible for me to be free."

"You're welcome, but it really is your right." Richard smiled. "Now what do you want to do today? Do you want to go into town and get the supplies you need?"

"I have to check on things here. I should have done it last night," Denny acknowledged. "At least turned the sprinklers on."

"In a while." Richard tipped his face up to the sun and closed his eyes. "We've got time. All the time in the world."

"Richard," Denny said very quietly after another long pause. "I want you to do something for me. I want you to stop putting money in my bank account."

"Why?" Richard's gaze was on Denny's face in a heartbeat. "Are you leaving?"

"Do you want me to?"

Richard looked away. "I knew you would eventually. It was too good to last and I've got no right to keep you here. I'm only a few years older than you but sometimes I feel about a hundred. You're young and free, you should be out there..." He pressed his lips together tightly, white outlining their edges, his hands twisting together in his lap.

"But do you want me to go?"

"No," Richard said simply.

"Good, because I don't want to either."

Turning quickly, Richard stared at him again. "Then why do you want me to stop the money?"

"Because it's not right. I shouldn't be paid for something I want to do." Denny tilted his head as he gazed over.

Richard carried on staring at him as though trying to understand.

"I just think it's time we stopped kidding ourselves," Denny said. "We both know I love you and I have for a while. Don't pay me for something I want to give you, something that's yours by right. I want to be here with you just because I want to and for no other reason."

Richard dragged in a breath, holding it as he scanned the rows of stakes set out across the land, looking at the small plants that were just starting to grow. "I love you too and—" He paused, exhaling noisily. "Wow, I thought that was going to be so hard to say, hard to admit, even to myself. Especially after Grady. But it's not." His gaze caught Denny's, holding fast. "I love you and it's easy and comfortable and feels... I don't know the word for it but right seems to work. It feels right."

"Right works for me as well," Denny said, acutely aware of where his knee touched Richard's. He didn't need to push into it, to make it anything more than it was, but that felt right as well. "So I stay just because it's what we want. There's no deal or job or anything else holding me here."

"Yeah." Richard breathed hard. "We," he whispered. "I'm part of a 'we' again. Without Grady. It's easier than I imagined."

"Is that okay?" The answer mattered so very much.

"Yeah." Richard nodded. "Grady would have approved."

"Good." Denny felt a knot of tension in his belly ease that he hadn't even known was there.

"We get a joint account instead," Richard added.

"Okay." Denny smiled gently, knowing all Richard was trying to say. "And Simms? What are you going to do about him?"

"Let him know it's not happening." A smile warmed Richard's eyes.

"Will that be a problem?"

"Not really. It was only ever an arrangement, never a passion."

"Are you sure? You were going to build alliances, help the movement."

"That was only possible when I thought there wasn't a chance of anything better, anything worth more."

"Are we're worth more?"

"Oh yes," Richard said in a voice so sincere it warmed something deep inside Denny. "What were you going to do if I said no to that question?"

"Smack you around the head until you saw sense." It was Denny's turn to grin. "I mean, I know you like to do the right thing and be all heroic and stuff but, come on, Ritchie, there are limits."

Richard's face seemed to soften at the abbreviation of his name. "You'd fight for me?" he asked.

"Against Simms? Hell yes. But I'd..." He dragged in a breath. "Yesterday I'd have walked into that knife for you, without even thinking about it first. You mean that much to me."

"When I saw him going for you..." Richard looked down at his hands. "I could have killed him. Probably would have if Harley hadn't stopped me. I couldn't lose you."

"Wow," Denny said. "This being-in-love business is heavy."

"Too heavy?"

"Not a chance," Denny said with a decisiveness he hadn't known he was capable of. "Are you okay? I mean, with all this? I know it's different for you. I thought you might freak when I said it, what with..."

"With Grady? Yeah, it is different. I didn't think it was possible to feel like this about anyone else, but I'm okay. Grady would have liked you. I don't think he would've understood you, but he'd have liked you."

"Why not understand me?"

Richard shrugged. "You're more easygoing than he was. You accept things, make compromises. Grady was a black-and-white kind of man."

"I can compromise on things that don't matter," Denny said, his tone measured. "But you matter.

You're an all-or-nothing man and I love that, I want that. I'm not going to compromise on you. If being free means I get to make decisions, decisions that can be scary, then I'm going to make the scariest one of my life. It would be so easy to accept what I could get here but..." He licked at his lips, the movement fast and furtive. "I don't want half measures with you. I want..." He stopped again and took a quick, harsh breath. "I want all or nothing. And I am shit-scared saying that." He finished with a lame laugh.

"You don't have to be." Richard glanced over at him, and again the warmth in his eyes made something in Denny's belly turn over. "I could have settled for less with someone else, at least I thought I could, but not with you. You've got all or nothing and I want, no, I'm going to demand the same from you."

"You've got it as well." Denny looked out over the land, the smile pulling at his face nowhere near enough to express half of what he felt. "You've got all of me, and there's a hell of a lot of it."

"I can handle that, but you have to be sure. Sure it's what you really want and sure... I can't think of a way to say this that doesn't sound patronizing so I'm sorry, I'm just going to say it. Are you sure about how you feel? You've only been free for five minutes. I'm the first person you've really got to know since then and I've helped you out, listened to you, fallen in love with you. It wouldn't be surprising if you..." He hitched a shoulder. "You know what I mean."

"If it was hero worship rather than love I felt?"

"Something like that."

"I'm not completely naïve. Slaves do have relationships as well, you know."

"I'm sorry," Richard said. "You admitted you were shit-scared demanding all or nothing. Well, I have to push this. I have to make sure, even if I hate what I find. You told me you made yourself stop loving people."

"I also told you I'd had sex with people I cared about."

"It's not the same as loving someone."

"You think I could have stopped myself if it was real?" Denny took a couple of deep breaths, picking up a stone and throwing it across the turned earth, gathering his thoughts as he watched it bounce. "Do you honestly think I wanted to fall for you? You were paying me. You could have thrown me out any time you wanted. Yeah, you were decent with me, but you're that way with everyone. I thought you saw me as exactly what you'd hired, a guy to do a job. I fell despite myself, because of who you are as a man. I love you for you and I do know what love is. But perhaps more important than all that, I know myself, as a slave you have to. I love you and it's real and honest and..." Another shrug. "Yours if you want it."

"I do want it," Richard said, voice small and nearly crippled with emotion. "I want it, all of it, but..." He turned, his gaze searching for Denny's. "You do understand why I had to make sure, don't you?"

"Yeah, I understand." Denny stared right back. "Because it's who you are, why I love you. You have to make sure everyone's safe and taken care of, even at a cost to you. But what about you? Are you sure you don't just think you feel that way because I'm the first person to get close to you and we have amazing sex?"

"It's not about the sex." The resolution was back in Richard's tone. "I've had a lot of offers over the last five years."

"But I'm the only one you took to bed?"

"It's not about sex or a good friendship. I can get both of those elsewhere, you know that. It's about..." He sucked in a long, deep breath. "It's about connection, a spark that suddenly lit. It's about me wanting you and not just in bed. I want you around. Here, now, like this. I wouldn't have said anything if it was just sex. I'm not built like that, you can take my word on it."

"I do. I know sex isn't that important to you." Denny cupped the side of Richard's face, at once both gentle and possessive. "I take your word on that, on everything else, and... Why don't we just stop talking now?"

"What else you got in mind?"

"Don't know." Denny stroked his thumb under Richard's eye. "Thought I might do this." He leaned in, licking across Richard's lips then leaving a line of small, soft kisses.

"It's a good start." Richard traced his tongue over the skin where Denny's had just been, chasing the taste. "You got anything else?"

"I was going to follow up with this." Denny tilted his head, lifting his other hand to frame Richard's face as he kissed again, deeper, wetter, slipping his tongue over Richard's, and opening his mouth wide. He pressed, wanting it all, everything, as he held Richard, pulling him closer. "Man, I thought you could kiss before" — he breathed against Richard's lips — "but it has nothing on this."

And it didn't. Admitting how he felt, knowing how Richard felt about him, ratcheted everything up to such a level that Denny felt like he was halfway drunk.

He kissed Richard again, slow and easy, realizing they really did have all the time in the world to just enjoy this. There was nothing waiting over the horizon to smack him back down, to rip this away from him. He knew Richard, trusted him down to his bones, and if Richard said all or nothing, all or nothing it would be.

He pushed his hands up into Richard's hair, sliding closer, the step digging into his ass forgotten as his senses filled with taste, smell, touch. With Richard.

"You want to take this back to the bedroom?" Richard asked, eyes gentle and hazy, mouth slack and just begging to be kissed once more.

"Yeah, just..." Denny leaned in again, pressing his tongue into Richard's mouth without even thinking about it, like it had a right to be there. Like it belonged.

He bit Richard's bottom lip, sucking it into his mouth and soothing it with his tongue, then he kissed Richard again.

It wasn't until Denny realized he was trying to climb into Richard's lap that he got his act together enough to move. Even then it was hard. How was he supposed to let go, even for a moment? But the lure of the bedroom, a flat surface, and a soft mattress was strong. In the end he hooked his hands in the waistband of Richard's sweatpants and simply dragged him along the hallway, mouths still pressed together, bodies closer than close. Even so they managed to get stuck in the bedroom door, shoulders and knees catching, until Denny pulled at Richard again.

"If you pick me up and carry me like a girl on her wedding night, I will beat you to a pulp like you deserve." Richard laughed, his eyes sparkling in ways Denny had never seen before.

"You could, too." Denny bit at Richard's neck. "I might be bigger but I've seen you fight. You could mash me without even trying." He stopped, hands on Richard's hips, face suddenly mock serious. "If I promise to fuck you so sweetly you forget everything except my name, will you promise not to turn me into baby food?"

"You're on." Richard's grin was bright and devastating.

Then, suddenly, he launched himself at Denny, pushing them both until they tumbled onto the bed in a mass of flailing limbs and laughter. Twisting and rolling, they fought for the top spot until Denny planted a hand on Richard's chest and just pressed, pinning him down with his body.

For a long moment Denny held still, simply looking down at Richard. Then he kissed him, his mouth warm and firm as he took his time. Again he cupped the side of Richard's face, fingertips in his hair, holding him steady. "I love you," he said. "And it really is as easy as that."

"So show me." Richard's eyes were round and open and honest, never leaving Denny's face.

Denny did, taking his time to stroke and touch and express things with his hands and mouth that just felt damned stupid when he tried to say them out loud.

When he finally pressed in, with Richard's knees drawn up and fallen wide to the sides, he felt strung out, ripped open with emotion and want. He wasn't going to let this go. The slick tight heat around his cock, the muscle and power under his hands, the need and trust in Richard's eyes. More than that, though, he wasn't going to let Richard down.

It was Grady Porter's Richard under him, sweating, pleading and biting his lip. He was buried balls-deep in Grady Porter's Richard and he was never going to forget that. Never going to forget who Richard was, what he stood for, and the chance he was taking.

Never going to forget the chance Richard had given him.

He fucked harder, with everything he had, panting fast as he fought with the need to get deeper, farther, more, all of Richard. He stretched down, needing to taste, hips still moving ruthlessly, until his mouth was against Richard's, then let it all go. Fucking until he didn't know where he ended and Richard began. Coming until Richard was full of him, the knowledge of that making him shatter and shake, collapsing down onto Richard.

"It's all right." Richard cradled him, a hand in his hair. "I've got you," words said over and over as Denny curled in tight, trembling.

Chapter Six

Harley turned up at the house in the early evening when Denny had finally decided it was time they got out of bed. Harley looked like he expected trouble, either to find it or be the cause of it. His face was tight and wary when he first saw Richard. "You all right?" he asked.

"Yeah," Richard said, grabbing a couple of beers and flopping down on a kitchen chair, scratching his belly. He pushed one over to Harley.

"Do you want to stay for something to eat?" Denny asked, smiling at Harley's uncertainty. "We don't have much but I can find something. Ritchie, we really need to go grocery shopping."

"Sure, thanks." Harley nodded. "Detlef sent the police into the town. He was really fucking annoyed that they'd pulled knives on us."

"It's not as if it hasn't happened enough times before." Richard shrugged.

"Detlef said he wanted to give a warning to everyone that if he sent people in, they were to stay safe and be respected. That we're his—and the movement's—representatives."

"Respected? Now that's almost funny."

"I think you made your point. That guy you slashed needed a hell of a lot of stitches in his face."

"What about his arm?"

"Well." Harley grinned. "I may have broken that."

"There wasn't any trouble, was there?" Denny asked, coming to stand behind Richard. "I mean, for taking me along or for the fight."

"Fuck no. The boss trusts us, trusts our judgment." Harley grinned again, wide and just a little bit devilish. "If there's a problem, Detlef always believes Richard over everyone else, and Richard's used that to his advantage enough times."

"So he should. Ritchie's very trustworthy. So can I go again?" Denny asked.

"Only if you either learn to fight or to keep out of it and—what the fuck is going on with you two?" Harley suddenly stopped, his gaze going back and forward between them.

"What?" Denny tensed.

"No one gets away with calling him Ritchie. He's only ever allowed it from me and Grady and you've just called him it twice."

Denny stood stock-still, staring just to the side of Harley's face but Richard didn't seem to have a problem looking straight at his best friend.

"Jesus H Christ," Harley said in amazement. He pushed the chair back, stretching his legs out, a grin just starting to form on his lips. "So you finally did it?" He nodded at Denny but his focus was on Richard. "You finally got your head out of your butt and admitted stuff? Took you fucking long enough."

"I'm glad you have such faith in me," Richard said levelly.

"So, it was the fight that gave you the kick in the ass to do it?"

"Sort of." Richard shrugged. "Not really. Denny told me he loved me."

"That's it? You couldn't have worked that out for yourself? Fucking hell, man, of course he does. Haven't you seen the way he's been drooling at you for the last few weeks?" Harley laughed. "And you love him, that's just as obvious."

"Yeah well, maybe it wasn't so blindingly obvious to me," Richard confessed. "It wasn't until he said it that I could admit what I already knew and —" He ground to a halt.

"Hold on a minute." Denny pulled out a chair, sitting close to Richard but aiming the question at Harley. "Are you telling me you knew?"

"It wasn't exactly hard." Harley was still smiling. "You get these big puppy-dog eyes whenever you look at Richard and you can't wait to get in his pants."

Denny dismissed that with a wave of his hand. He really didn't want to think about being that easy to read. He never used to be. "But you knew how Richard felt?"

"The stupid fucker might not be able to admit things to himself but I know him better than anyone. I was waiting to see what would happen when he came around to the idea. By the state of you two I'm guessing you spent the day in bed."

Denny reddened but carried on. "You're okay with it?"

"Why wouldn't I be? I already told you if you hurt him I'll kill you. That still stands. Only now you know I really can do it."

"But he's…" Denny looked at Richard. "He's who he is."

"Listen." Harley was serious again. "If you make him happy then everything's fine by me. He deserves some good times." He stared at Richard, eyes just as serious. "I kept telling you to move on and Simms, or anyone like him, was a bad idea. If Tassel Boy is the one that does it for you, then grab him. Apart from his god-awful taste in jackets, I like him. This is right, it's good, and I'll defend you two to hell and back. Just promise me you'll let yourself enjoy it."

"Thanks, man," Richard said quietly. "I will."

"Are we going to need defending?" Denny asked, glancing between the two men. "Or do we just keep it real quiet?"

Richard reached over to rest a hand on the back of Denny's neck, squeezing gently and running a thumb into his hair. "I'm not hiding what we have. I'm proud of us. Anyone who doesn't like it, well, that's their problem."

"Now that we've got all that crap settled." Harley's grin was firmly back in place. "Am I going to get fed or are you going to tell me how great the sex is first? Details, guys. I want details."

Much later, Denny sat next to Richard on the sofa with the guitar perched on his knee, waiting for Harley to get extra beer from his car. Richard's arm was around him, guiding his hands on the strings. He bowed his head closer to Richard's, concentrating hard. Suddenly he looked up, laughing at his own mistake. But then he was caught by Richard's gaze, the happiness shining in his eyes. He reached over to touch Richard's face, just resting his fingertips against his cheek, before leaning in to kiss him. It was just a soft brushing of lips but Denny couldn't stop his eyes closing.

He pulled away first, his tongue lapping at his own lips as his gaze stayed on Richard's mouth for a moment more. Then he nudged Richard and their attention went back to the guitar.

"Goddamn it, but you two are cute," Harley said, startling them. "Not that I ever thought I'd call a man like you, Ritchie, cute. Not one that can fight like you. But fuck, being happy suits you." He pointed at Denny, grinning. "You, Tassel Boy, turned out to be an okay kind of guy. We struck really lucky with you. You're good for Richard, and it seems like Richard is good for you too. Hell, it's like that whole 'the sum being more than its parts' thing." Harley grinned wider, as though proud of himself for thinking of the analogy. "You know, maybe it's time I find myself a nice girl. Although, I figure I won't go about it quite the way Richard did."

Richard actually blushed and Denny threw a cushion at Harley.

* * * *

A week or so later Denny woke slowly, the world starting to encroach into his sleep with a pleasing reality. The mattress was soft and the cover warm. God, he loved this bed with the smell of maleness ingrained into the sheets. He pressed his nose against the pillow. Richard and him, man and sex. Best fragrance he'd ever smelled. He loved the scent, the bed, the room, the house. He stretched, back arching, arms high over his head, toes pointing to the wall, smile curling at his lips.

Fucking amazing bed.

He rubbed a hand over his face, up into his hair, before rolling over. He didn't have to go far before he was pushing into Richard's comforting mass. Richard, all warm and snuggly and sleep-soaked. He wasn't totally sure if Richard would like being thought of as snuggly, but hell, the guy was asleep. He wasn't about to do any complaining. And he sure did smell nice. Man and sweat and muscles and...muscles didn't smell.

Denny grinned and pushed in closer. Richard didn't even stir so he slipped a hand over his waist, palm flat on his belly. Muscles, man, sex. Life didn't get much better than that. As he drew small circles against the warm flesh, Denny's grin changed. He could bring Richard off, slow and easy, make him all relaxed and open, then he could take his time fucking him senseless. Or fucking until he himself was senseless.

He cupped Richard's balls for a moment, just enjoying the weight of them in his hand. Man, every bit a man. He rolled them, feeling the changing texture and solidity, before sliding his hand up. Richard was already hard for him. He rubbed, just a couple of times, just so he could feel the drag of silky flesh against his hand, before he spat on his fingers. Then back and...oh, that slide felt good. Richard's cock seemed to be made to fit right there, right in the palm of his hand.

He squeezed once and Richard huffed, his shoulder hitching back against Denny. That seemed to know where it fit as well. Slow and steady, it seemed like a morning set for a pace like that. Build it easy, let Richard glide into his hand, no work for anyone. Just a gentle, perfect pace.

Richard shivered, twitching as he made a mumbled, questioning noise that wasn't really a word. Denny took it as a sign of encouragement or enjoyment or something. He stroked again and again, pressing into Richard's back, digging his nose into his neck. This was going faster than he'd intended. Already he could feel the exaggerated expansion of Richard's chest, the quickening of his breath that meant things were close. Oh well, so be it. If that's what Richard—or Richard's body—wanted, then that was more than fine.

Placing a kiss on Richard's shoulder, he tightened his grip, going a little faster, making each pull count just that little bit more. Again Richard shivered as his hips thrust forward into Denny's hand. Faster, always a bit faster. Denny kept his open mouth pressed to Richard's skin, his hand learning the pace Richard wanted, needed.

Richard arched back, body pushing into Denny's, mouth soft with gratification, body trembling with each pull and twist of Denny's hand. He moaned, high and cracked, the sound seemingly dragged from somewhere inside him. Eyes squeezed tightly shut, he stretched his neck as his head pushed against Denny in a silent plea for more, now, release. Denny licked up the long column of pale skin, deliberately catching his tongue on the day-old stubble. Richard moaned again, almost broken, his head falling forward. Denny loved that sound.

"Almost there," Denny murmured on warm flesh. "Come on, let it go." He moved his hand, not harder, but faster, squeezing at the tip and base repeatedly as he coiled around and over Richard.

He kept up the relentless pressure, leaving no room for Richard to catch his breath. No time, no space. Get the burn to start in his balls and… Richard came into Denny's hand with yet another moan. Richard curled in on himself, face buried in his own arm, eyes still shut tightly as Denny stroked him gently through it.

"A good one, yeah?" Denny dropped a couple of kisses onto Richard's shoulder. "I felt that one shake right through you." Two more gentle strokes and he wiped his hand on Richard's belly before lifting it to his mouth to taste his fingers.

Richard breathed fast and hard, face still hidden.

"I reckon we're getting so good at this, you and me together" — Denny slid back, trying to roll Richard so he could kiss him — "that we should start making educational DVDs. You know, to teach lesser mortals how good it can be. What do you think?" He pressed a hand on Richard's chest, fingers stroking, encouraging him to move.

But before Denny had a chance to stop him he felt Richard tense and the next moment he was up out of bed, standing with his shoulders drooped, his back to Denny.

"Hey, get back here." Denny laughed. "I'm not finished with you yet."

But Richard was already reaching for any clothes he could find, not saying a word.

"What are you doing?" Denny asked, all humor gone from his voice.

Richard pulled on jeans and Denny's T-shirt.

"Ritchie?"

Richard grabbed his shoes and headed for the door.

"Don't you fucking walk out on me, not like this," Denny called, a trace of fear in his voice. "If you've got a problem, talk to me."

Richard stopped, hand already on the doorknob, and turned. But his gaze didn't make it to the bed. "I..." He licked frantically at his lips. "I can't." Then he was off down the hallway.

"Richard," Denny yelled after him. "Don't do this. Tell me what I did wrong."

But Richard was already gone, the car starting up with a roar of the engine and a spray of gravel as it pulled away quickly.

Denny kept calling Richard's phone all morning, ignoring the 'person is unavailable' message, knowing that sooner or later Richard would calm down and explain what the fuck was going on. By lunchtime he was beginning to think it wouldn't be quite as easy as that. He kept replaying the scene in bed over and over in his mind. It was no good. He couldn't work out what he'd said or done wrong, but he wasn't about to give up. No way. He called again.

It wasn't until about two in the afternoon that the phone rang. Of course, Denny was in the bathroom at the time and the answering machine had kicked in before he could get to it. He shouldn't have bothered running. It was Harley on the other end.

"You there, Tassel Boy? I don't know what the hell's going on but Richard asked me to let you know he's okay and he'll be back later. Fuck knows why he couldn't tell you himself, but don't worry. Even if I have to break every bone in his body, I'll beat some sense into him and send him home. You're the best thing that's happened to him since...since I can't remember when."

Denny exhaled slowly, picked up the phone, said a brief, "Thanks," to Harley, who was still talking to the machine, and replaced it again. Then he went back to waiting.

He was sitting at the kitchen table late that evening, nursing his second glass of whiskey, when he heard the car pull up slowly outside. He didn't move, didn't react other than to twirl the liquid around in his glass, watching it intently. Eventually Richard came in, standing in the doorway for a moment, bottom lip caught between his teeth. Then he dropped his keys and sat opposite Denny. He poured out a single measure then knocked it back before looking at Denny properly. His mouth opened but then he stopped, no words coming out.

Denny didn't like the silence.

"I didn't deserve that," Denny said levelly. "I didn't deserve this morning. If you have a problem, you tell me. How else am I supposed to know what I did wrong?"

"You didn't do anything wrong." Richard laid out the words carefully.

"Yeah?" Denny raised his eyebrow sharply. "Then how come you ran away from me? I thought we were trying for something good here. Is that how you always act or have you changed your mind about me, us?"

"I haven't changed my mind. I..." Richard stared down at the chipped wood of the table top. It was scarred and flawed. "I'm sorry I ran. That wasn't fair to you."

"Too right it wasn't. So what was it?" Denny's lips were strained tight. "What did I do?"

"I already said—nothing." Richard got up, rooting around on the counter as though trying to find something to occupy his hands.

"If not me, then what?"

Richard straightened the coffee jar, lined up a row of mugs, chewed at his lip, and said nothing.

"Talk to me. Fucking talk to me." Denny's patience snapped. "We don't stand a chance otherwise."

"I know, I know." Richard took a ragged breath and turned around slowly. "I want..." Then the words ran out again.

"What do you want?"

"I..."

Denny shook his head. "Why is this so hard? I don't get it. You've always been able to talk to me, right from the start. I know all your secrets, so what's the big deal?"

"I don't know where to start, how to tell you, what to say." Richard pressed his back into the kitchen counter as though he needed it to keep him grounded.

"Try at the beginning," Denny said, harsher than he meant to. He sucked in a breath at the expression of panic on Richard face and started again. "Okay, we were in bed, I was jacking you off and you seemed like you were enjoying it and... Were you enjoying it? Have I got that wrong? Fuck, can't I read you as well as I thought I could?"

"Yeah, I was enjoying it." Richard wouldn't look at him again. "It was..."

"Fuck it, talk to me." Denny wasn't sure if he was shouting or pleading as he spread his hands wide. "I was jacking you. I know we haven't done that before but we've fucked enough times. It can't be a big deal."

Only it was, and the moment the words were out of Denny's mouth, Richard's expression changed, tightening, flushing, looking more uncomfortable than a man had a right to.

"Dear God, what the hell is it?" Denny got up, pushing his way into Richard's space, crowding him, making him face this. Making him talk. Pinning him in place with an arm on either side of Richard's body.

But Richard still didn't seem ready, twisting and turning as though he'd bolt again if he could. "You were jacking me and…"

"If you didn't like it you should have said."

"But I did, I did." Richard managed to get his focus on Denny again, and the look in them was begging Denny to understand. "It felt good and right and—"

"What's the problem then? You've done it before, you said you had." Denny grabbed onto Richard's belt. He fucking wasn't going to let him run. He didn't know why but he did know this was way too important for that.

"That's the problem."

"What?"

"I have done it before. I did it all the time. It was just about the only thing I did with…"

"Oh." Denny caught his breath, realization dawning. Yeah, of course. "Grady."

"Yeah, Grady." Richard's face had softened but the panic hadn't gone.

"It's what you did with him. I reminded you of him, made you think of him. Of course you freaked."

"No." Richard coiled his hand in Denny's T-shirt, his nails scraping the skin underneath.

"Then what?" Denny asked gently. Once more, Richard's face had twisted up and he wasn't speaking. "It wasn't like it was with him? It didn't feel as good?"

"It did." Pain and horror and God knew what else chased themselves across Richard's face. "It felt good. It felt…better." Suddenly Richard sagged, needing firm hands to stop him falling as, for a brief moment, Denny thought he was going to cry. "The only thing I did with him, all I had of him in the last years, and it was better with you. But I've only known you a few months and…" Then there were tears, only a few, but

Denny saw them as he tried to pull Richard in toward his body. At first Richard resisted, betrayal clouding his expression, before he gave in and buried his face against Denny's neck.

"Ritchie," Denny whispered, stroking his hands across Richard's back, aware of the shape and texture of the scars through the thin material of his shirt. "I'm sorry. I don't know what to say to you. I'm so sorry and I don't even know what I'm sorry about." He hugged tighter, letting Richard lean on and into him. "I'm sorry he was hurt so bad, that you never got more together, that it was stolen from you both. I'm so sorry he died." He pressed an almost chaste kiss to the side of Richard's head, drawing in a breath and Richard's smell. "But I'm not sorry I've got you. I'll never be sorry about that."

"When... We... I..." Richard started each sentence but couldn't finish any of them, straightening up instead. He looked awful, face pulled tight, drained of color, eyes surrounded by dark smudges of black. "I'm sorry I ran, that I hurt you. I didn't mean that. I woke up and it was you and—" He sucked in another huge gulp of air. "Sorry."

"It doesn't matter. None of that matters."

"I panicked and the next thing I knew I was in the car and... I didn't know what to say or how to say it and I got scared," Richard admitted.

"Don't be scared." Denny hung onto his sleeve, not ready to let go yet. "But talk to me, always remember that."

"Talk to the man I currently love about the one I...?"

"About the one you still love," Denny said with complete certainty, digging his fingers deeper into Richard's clothes. "I know you love him, that you always will. It makes you who you are. He's part of you. I don't want that to change because of us, that wouldn't be right. Fuck it, man. I've never thought about 'doing the right thing'. Not until I met you. That's your doing, and Grady's. Don't change now."

"You sure?"

"Yes, damn you." Denny smiled. He meant it. By fuck he meant it.

"Talk to you about anything?"

"Yes."

"Even when I have no idea what I want to say or how I feel?"

"Yeah, even then." Denny pulled him in for a brief hug, knowing they might both be as confused as hell but at least they were on the right track. He wiped a thumb across Richard's cheek, cupping his face. "It's not all you had of him, it's not. You know that, don't you?"

"I guess." Richard scratched at his head, fingers too rough, too hard.

"What people do in bed doesn't mean a thing. Trust me I know. You know it as well."

"But..." Richard whispered.

"No, listen." Denny was very nearly tempted to shake him. "When you wake up in the morning with a hangover and your hair's all over the place and you look like shit, the first thing you do is search around until you see me and then your face kind of lights up. It may be fucking girly, mushy shit, but that means more than you shouting my name when I fuck you. Anyone can do sex. It's all the other stuff that really matters. And you had that by the truckload with Grady."

For the first time since he'd walked back into the house, Richard's face began to truly soften and the tension eased from his back. Maybe his smile didn't cover all the pain on his face but it did make it to his eyes, and that was what Denny thought really mattered.

Denny pulled him into yet another hug and this time Richard melted against him.

* * * *

Back at the bar a couple of nights later, Denny watched from the comfort of a corner table as Richard made the rounds again, chatting with friends, laughing and joking. He was doing better, much better, but Denny knew the freak out over the hand job had really hit him hard. Soul searching about Grady was something Richard simply wasn't used to.

Richard was sure about Grady, always had been completely and utterly sure. Denny had managed to convince him what had happened didn't matter, didn't reflect on anything, but...Denny hadn't attempted a repeat performance and Richard wasn't talking about it.

Richard had temporarily lost a little of his innate self-assurance and Denny was reminded yet again just how much Grady was a part of him. Did it matter? Denny had thought of him as 'Grady Porter's Richard' right from the start. Of course it didn't matter. It was who he was.

It also didn't hurt his own confidence that Richard kept looking over, not constantly, but enough quick glances that Denny felt sure Richard always knew where he was. Little glances with a furtive smile and a softness to his eyes.

"You sorted him out then." Harley slapped Denny hard enough on the back that he had to stop himself from sliding off his chair.

"Yeah, I hope so." Denny nodded as Harley sat next to him.

"Good. That's good." They both watched Richard across the room. "He doesn't show it, but he's been miserable for a long time. Got himself ingrained into it until he couldn't see any other way. You've given him a second chance, just—"

"I know," Denny interrupted, smiling into his beer. "Don't hurt him or you'll kill me. And I do know it's not an idle threat."

"Well, that's true." Harley cocked his head to the side. "But it wasn't what I was going to say."

"You were going to describe the method of my demise? Beheading? Impaling? A long slow death by killer bees?"

"Killer bees? Man, you're odd. I could come up with a damned sight worse than killer bees." Both of Harley's eyebrows rose as he pulled a face. "I was going to say you're good for him but—"

"What?"

"You've made him vulnerable. He can get hurt now in ways he was completely shut off to before."

"I'm not going to hurt him," Denny said with certainty.

Harley looked at him long and appraisingly while Denny held still under the scrutiny. "I think you'll do everything you can to protect him, and not because of my threats. But I also think he can hurt himself. Is that what happened?"

"Sort of," Denny admitted.

"Grady?"

"Yeah."

"He's always going to feel guilty over Grady."

"Why? It wasn't Richard's fault Grady died."

"No, but he lived and Grady's dead. There's enough guilt in that to last a lifetime."

"Then I guess I have to convince him to put it to one side and be happy." Denny fixed his attention back on Richard.

"Oh, he is happy." Harley slapped him on the back again, just as forcefully. "Trust me, he's happy. He's just taking a bit of time getting used to the idea."

As they watched, Richard glanced over again, quickly assessing the situation before heading their way. "Look at you two, getting along like regular friends with no fighting or threats or shouting." He slid in close to Denny, their thighs pressing together. "There weren't any threats, were there?"

"He was going on about killer bees but there were no threats from me." Harley was all sweet and innocent. "We were just having a nice, intelligent conversation."

"Were you talking about me?" Richard narrowed his eyes.

"Why would we do that?" Denny leaned in, turning his whole body toward Richard. "We've got better things to talk about than you."

"Like what?"

"Killer bees," Harley and Denny said in unison, then laughed, long and loud, at Richard's confused face.

"Fucking idiots," Richard complained as he reached in to brush fluff from Denny's face, his fingers lingering.

"Got yourself someone new, Richard?" came a woman's alcohol-blurred voice. "What's the matter, Grady's memory not enough for you anymore?"

"Leave it alone, Stella," Harley snapped. "Grady's been dead five years."

"So? Richard here is our very pretty poster boy for the Grady Porter fan club. Can't have him spoiling that just because he's got a fancy for some young cock."

"Shut your mouth, bitch." Harley pushed his chair back when he stood. "I don't care how drunk you are, this is none of your business." The lower his voice dropped, the more menacing he became. Stella looked down at Richard as the room went silent behind her and all eyes turned to watch. "I thought we had you lined up for Simms. I hear that's off and I can see why now. But we all have to play our part."

"Haven't I already done that?" Richard said, his voice measured and controlled. "I gave everything until I had nothing left. Surely that's enough?"

"So now you keep up appearances. You're Grady's heartbroken widow and you're meant to stay that way."

"Richard isn't anybody's anything." Another voice entered the fray as Detlef Meyer came to stand behind Denny and Richard. He rested a hand on both of their shoulders. "That's what we fought for, Stella. The right for us all to be free."

"He can do what he likes in private." She raised a hand in an indifferent gesture. "Fuck who he likes. But in public he should have the grieving face and mournful eyes."

"He's done enough already. More than you have," Detlef said, and there was no way anyone would have the guts to argue with his tone. "You're important to the peace, he fought the war. You wouldn't be here without him and you'd do well to remember that. Richard deserves any happiness he can find and I wish him all the luck in the world."

"But the pressure is still on. We're not finished yet. We all have to make sacrifices," she went on.

"He's made enough and we don't need what you're asking of him," Detlef said. "Now this conversation is finished. Wish Richard well and walk away. You've got a life, he gets one as well."

She shrugged, face scrunching up as she deferred to Detlef. "If you think so." She nodded at Richard, offering a slurred "Good luck" before she turned and left.

"Are you all right?" All eyes remained on them when Detlef looked pointedly at Richard.

"Yeah, but are you sure about this?" Richard licked at his lips as uncertainty clouded his face. "I mean, Stella has a point. We all need to keep a public face. I'm not giving Denny up but we can hide it, we don't have to—"

"Richard," Detlef said firmly. "You know I don't lie, not to any of you. Not many people are lucky enough to find something good, let alone twice. I meant what I said to Stella. You deserve a life. Take the chance you've got and make one." Then he turned just as decisively toward Denny and offered his hand. "It's Denny, isn't it?"

"Yes," Denny replied, reaching out. "It's an honor to meet you properly."

"It's an honor to meet you, too. Anyone who can make Richard smile again has to be one of the good guys. I've known him over ten years and he's never done it enough." Detlef pulled up a chair. "You want another beer?"

The room slowly came back to life around them as Denny finally got to know his hero.

Chapter Seven

Denny drove his new-old truck through the security gate then pulled up next to Richard's car. His truck. His new truck that he'd had exactly three days. All right, so maybe it was as old as the hills and only held together by rust and extra rivets, but it was new to him and all his. Bought with money he'd earned.

Sort of.

Mostly it was money raised from selling his first harvest. Something that had made his belly twist with an emotion he wouldn't admit was pride. But he'd seen Richard sneak off with the car lot owner, a hand casually resting on his shoulder. When they'd wandered back, the price had been miraculously reduced to one he could actually afford.

He'd repaid Richard for that, but not between the sheets. Oh no, that he did purely for free. Because he wanted to. Because he couldn't get enough.

Richard, who'd had so many 'touching issues' back at the start. He sure as hell didn't have them now, grabbing onto Denny as hard, tightly and frequently as he could. He made Denny plead and beg unashamedly as he reached desperately to touch back. Just imagine, back then, Denny had thought Richard was unresponsive. Man, that was so untrue now as to be laughable. He shivered and shook under Denny's hands and tongue, twisted and squirmed on his cock.

Yeah, their sex life was something pretty amazing, but so were a lot of other things. Sitting opposite at the table eating as their gazes caught. Sharing a beer, watching the sun go down over all Denny's hard work. Driving into another town, another situation, next to each other, before Richard—and maybe Harley—would try to put things right. Even Denny had learned to help. Walking or standing side by side, shoulder to shoulder…yeah it was good. So was lying in bed together, head on chest, hand in hair, talking about the past and the future, love and hope.

No, Richard wasn't unresponsive anymore.

Maybe they didn't shout what they had from the rooftops but they didn't hide it either. Discreet, a good middle ground, one they could both live with, feel comfortable with. And if Richard's hand felt good at the small of Denny's back in the bar, so did his on Richard's shoulder as they walked back to the car.

"Ritchie," Denny called, going inside.

"In here." Richard's voice came from the kitchen. He glanced up from where he was crouched on the floor, retrieving dropped mail. A smile curled his lips as Denny dumped his packages on the table.

"Hi." Denny stopped and looked, almost taken aback by the peace and contentment in Richard's eyes, by his own reaction to it.

"Hi yourself. A good trip?"

"Yeah. The truck didn't break down all the way to the store and back."

"That's a first." Richard's smile grew, slowly and easily.

"Come to bed?" Denny suddenly asked, the question out there before he'd really thought about it.

"To celebrate the truck working? That's a lame excuse, man."

"Don't need an excuse. I just want to...with you... I just want," Denny finished, shrugging. Even he knew that really was lame.

"What's made you so mushy?" Richard stood up, already moving toward the door.

"Just happy. Is that okay?" Denny caught him at the end of the bed, turning him so they were facing each other.

"More than okay." Richard traced the line of Denny's jaw with his fingertips, laughing as he moved over lips and nose before stretching up to kiss him.

Denny loved that, loved that big, strong, I-helped-save-the-world-but-mushy-inside Grady Porter's Richard had to stretch up and tip his head back to kiss him. It made him want to take and keep and love and... He kissed back, giving all he could, matching Richard knee-melting touch for touch.

Denny feasted on Richard's lips. Taking and giving in equal parts, every inch man for man in a contest with no losers. He gripped Richard's belt at the back, holding him tightly, sliding his other hand down inside, into the warmth. "Bed now," he whispered into Richard's mouth.

"Yeah," came Richard's muffled reply, lips slick and puffy.

Next thing he knew they were naked on the bed. Denny pressed Richard back against the headboard with a kiss as deep as any he'd ever given before. Deep and long and slow. He pushed in between

Richard's thighs, cocks rubbing until Richard had to pull away to catch his breath.

Denny looked again. Richard's eyes were dark with need, heavy-lidded and full of intent. His face—one he could keep so stonily blank when he needed to—was open and full of a longing that was tinged with just a little desperation. Denny knew all about Richard's desperation. That feeling made him cling onto Denny when he was drunk, mumbling forgotten words about 'can't lose you' and 'not again'. Words remembered and repeated when he thought Denny was asleep.

"I want..." Denny kissed him again and again, stopping with his lips barely brushing Richard's. "I want..."

"So take." Richard nipped at Denny's lip.

"No." Denny shook his head softly. "Not this time. Now I want..." He wriggled himself up and around until he straddled Richard's lap with Richard pressed into the huge pile of pillows.

"You want me to?"

"Yeah." As much as Denny loved to fuck—Richard spread out under him, legs pushed wide, eyes fixed on his—this was something different, special. This was his alone. Richard had never fucked anyone but him, and Denny meant to keep it that way.

"Okay." He knew Richard understood exactly what it meant, even though they didn't talk about it. There was a huge difference between an 'I want to be fucked open and hard' fuck and an 'I need to be fucked by you' fuck. Denny pushed the lube into Richard's hand, grinning.

One finger, two. All the while, Denny mapped Richard's skin, covering everything he could reach. He stretched over, lapping and licking at Richard's mouth, his hips rising and falling on Richard's hand, going a little too fast.

Richard went to push in a third finger, his other hand jerking through the slick on Denny's cock, but Denny pushed down hard.

"Don't bother." Denny breathed hotly and desperately against Richard's lips. "I don't need it. I need you." He knew Richard understood this as well, his need to go close to pain in a quest for more, further, everything.

No one was getting hurt, but Denny had a need like a red haze that misted his eyes, clouded his judgment and burned in his veins. But he trusted Richard to keep them on the right side of the line.

Richard pushed in again, opening the way, and lifted Denny up a little higher. "Whatever you want." He kissed Denny, tongue pressing in deep as Denny aligned himself and took control.

Both caught their breath when Denny slid down, chests heaving at the sensation. Richard's breath stuttered, catching in his throat. "This feeling, being inside you. I know it now but...after, I can never remember just how good it is. This connection, this..."

"The awe and magnificence that takes your breath away?" Denny tried to laugh but it was all too much, too good.

"Something like that." Richard held on tighter as his breathing became more erratic.

Denny dictated the first few rises and falls, milking Richard's cock, reveling in a pleasure that would never get commonplace or be taken for granted. He started sighing into each glide, breath blending to match Richard's until they were in time, unified in a circle of satisfaction that had no beginning or end.

Slowly, the first wave of Richard's mumbled 'Yes' and 'Oh God' eased and he caught hold of Denny's hips, stilling them at the top of the rise when he thrust up into him. "Oh, fuck...that's so good. So sweet." Richard arched up, his feet pressing flat into the mattress as he fucked harder.

Denny couldn't help but buck with the first hard thrust. As he leaned forward he rested his forearms on Richard's shoulders, digging his hands into his hair. A shiver forced its way up his spine, making him clutch tighter, pant harder into Richard's mouth. "More," he demanded.

"Whatever you want," Richard said again, voice husky and dark. Again and again he thrust up, meeting and matching Denny stroke for stroke, all Denny wanted, needed but...

Denny forced his eyes open, drawing a harsh breath in through his nose. Much as he wanted to lay back and savor the feeling, he had to see this. He squeezed Richard's cock, upping the pace, knowing, trusting that Richard would...at the right second Richard would know what Denny needed from him.

Richard did. Just at that moment when Denny needed him most, Richard opened his eyes and Denny stared directly into them.

Two more thrusts, timing slightly off but not mattering in the least, and Richard was coming. His mouth hung open, slack and heavy, breath dragging in his chest. Denny tightened his hands in his hair as he slowly milked every last shudder and twitch from Richard.

"Yes," he hissed, resting his mouth against Richard's. "Yeah."

He kept his hips moving, no grand push, more a slight rocking that kept him aware, kept him feeling, again trusting that Richard would know what he wanted next. He wasn't wrong. Richard slid his hand from Denny's hip to smooth up his cock, grip immediately tight, pace immediately rapid.

Richard's fingers felt perfect on him and Denny arched back into all the sensations, trying to feel more of the cock still in his ass. Pull and twist, hard and fast, and he was coming, the movement of Richard's hand echoing through his body.

"Oh fuck, oh shit." Denny blew out breath after breath, face pressed into Richard's shoulder, body collapsing down as all the tension left his body at once.

"I've got you." Richard stroked up his spine when he eased out of Denny's body and pulled them even closer together.

"Yeah, you well and truly have." Denny laughed, soft and muzzy. He burrowed in deeper, before he changed his mind and kissed Richard deeply and wetly. "Shit, all I want to do now is roll over and start again."

"And your problem with that plan is what?" Richard tried to push Denny onto his back.

"Problem is I have to check outside. Water and put things away before I can call it a night." He dragged himself up, stretching protesting muscles when he bent to find his clothes.

"Can't it wait?" Richard leaned back against the headboard, contentment radiating from every pore.

"Nope. Not if I want anything to still be alive tomorrow. Give me an hour, two at the most, and I'll have you screaming my name."

"Cocky bastard." Richard swung his legs off the bed. "Okay, I have a pile of mail to check and then I'll fix us something to eat."

"You? Cook? God help us." Denny grinned as he ducked away from the inevitable shoe Richard threw at him. It wasn't so much that Richard was a terrible cook, it was just that Denny was better. A lot better.

Outside the sun was starting to dip, the heat of the afternoon easing to leave a glorious warmth in the air and the earth. Denny loved this time of day. It didn't feel as hectic as earlier but it was still full of promise. He looked over the land and smiled. He'd done well, created something out of nothing, and that made him feel good. He was proud of what he'd achieved. Proud of the soil under his boots and the leaves he could run his hand through.

Maybe it wasn't all he dreamed about. Maybe, possibly, one day they could have somewhere nearer the mountains. A bigger piece of land where they could raise some animals as well, cows or perhaps a few horses. He knew about horses, would love to work with them. Maybe. One day. But for now this was a good place to be, to learn how to do things his way, with no one to tell him.

No one to tell him. Just someone to share with.

He smiled, rubbing a hand over the back of his neck, then went to work. He started at the far edge, working his way back toward the house, the sun on his back was enough to make him sweat comfortably. He labored hard, feeling the burn in his muscles and the ache in his spine but in a good way. A way that made him feel satisfied and alive. An hour or so later and he was near the house. It was then he first heard the scream.

A sharp, harsh sound, one he couldn't place, couldn't recognize. It couldn't be real, could it? Couldn't be...human?

A sound so terrifying, so brutal and unearthly, that it couldn't be genuine. He stood listening. That was nothing like the screams he'd heard on TV shows or in the movies. That was full of excruciating, agonizing pain. That was...real.

He ran faster than he'd ever run before, feet pounding in the dirt as he banged through the door, the noise getting louder around his ears as he skidded into the kitchen.

Empty.

Living room.

Richard... Alive. Okay. Not hurt. Not the one screaming. On the floor, his back to Denny, on his knees in front of the television, hands pressing, pressing, pressing too hard into the screen. On the screen...

Dear God.

Inhuman.

Evil.

Denny's belly clenched and for a moment he rode the heaving as he fought not to throw up, the blood draining from his face as fast as the bile rose.

On the screen, Grady Porter. Naked and screaming. Dying. Blood and guts and bone.

Deliberate torture. Absolute evil.

On the screen, Grady Porter. Dead.

On the floor, Richard. On his knees and broken.

Denny stood fixed in place by the sheer horror. His gaze on the screen, on Richard's hands scratching at the glass, clawing, trying to get to Grady, trying to...

Then the DVD clicked off and the TV went blank and it was Richard screaming. Screaming Grady's name, trying to get him back, to bring him back but... No, not like that. Not that mangled wreckage. Remnants of flesh and guts.

Suddenly Denny came to life again. Richard, get to Richard. Help him, stop him from screaming. Do something, anything. Help somehow.

He made it to the TV, dropping down next to Richard, forcing Richard's hands away from the DVD player. "No, no. Don't watch it again, you can't."

"Grady." The word was more like a wail, drawn from Richard's very soul as he knocked Denny away, reaching for the machine again.

"No." Denny came back at him, grabbing at the cable and pulling it out the back when Richard wouldn't let him close. "Don't watch."

Richard stopped then, defeated by the inescapable. His gaze went from the ends of the disconnected wires to Denny's face, and Denny reeled back at the sight. He'd never seen such pain. It was deeper, more total than anything he'd ever imagined possible. All Richard's emotions, often so tightly bound, were now splayed open wide and pulsing.

That look would stay with Denny for more years than he could imagine.

"Grady," Richard said again, and this time it was a whisper drowning in hurt and longing. Then Richard was up and running, across the room and out of the door.

Denny grabbed his phone and was after him in a heartbeat.

Richard ran to the middle of the open space behind the house and stopped, desperately staring around him, as though trying to find somewhere to go, somewhere to hide. But Denny knew there would be no hiding from the pain on the TV screen. There'd be no getting away from that.

Richard seemed to know it as well as he leaned back, arms spread wide, and howled at the sky.

The sound gnawed into Denny's skin and bones, every bit as hard as Grady's screams.

He hit speed dial on his phone. "Harley, get here now."

Then he went after Richard once more. Only Richard was moving again, running toward the front of the house, and oh fuck, if he made it out of the gate Denny didn't know where he'd go. He ran, knowing Richard wasn't even aware of him.

Keep him in sight, follow but let him run, let him burn some of this…burn off some of the pain. Just follow, follow, follow. It didn't matter where they went as long as he didn't lose Richard.

Lose Richard.

He picked up his pace, lungs straining with the effort.

But Richard didn't make it out of the gate. As he rounded the edge of the house he misjudged the distance or didn't see or plain didn't know what he was doing. He crashed into the side of the outbuilding, the force knocking him off his feet. He came back up in a rush and it was as though the old building were personally responsible for everything that had happened. His hands clenched into fists, and the next second Richard was pounding at the wooden wall, smashing into it with every ounce of strength he had, over and over as Denny came up alongside him.

"Stop," he said lamely, knowing how useless it sounded.

Richard spared him a glance, and oh God, if that first look at his face had been awful, this was even worse. Hurt and hopelessness, pain and searing rage, and… Denny couldn't even begin to catalog all the other emotions that were now splattered with flecks of blood from Richard's hands, before he turned away again. Richard stared at the damaged wall almost as though he didn't recognize it before suddenly kicking out at it, attacking it with hands and feet and everything he had.

Denny stood and watched, not knowing what else to do. He'd heard Grady's screams, had seen the last few minutes of the DVD. He could feel his own rage and pain. But Richard had seen more, had seen it all. How would he feel if it weren't Grady torn and broken? If it were Richard screaming like that, Richard ripped apart and dead?

He threw up right where he stood, not bothering to step away. Then he watched while Richard used up the last of his strength until he crumpled to his knees in the dirt. Denny wiped ineffectually at his mouth as he too dropped down and crawled over.

He pulled Richard to him, and mercifully, Richard came, body limp but shaking right down to its core. Denny wrapped him tight as he could, holding him close as he could, hands fisted in Richard's clothes as Richard's shaking grew. Huge shudders racked Richard's body, making his shoulders heave and his legs tremble. Denny gripped harder, pressing his face into Richard's hair when Richard leaned into him.

That was where they were when Harley arrived an indeterminable amount of time later. Still sprawled out in the dirt, covered with blood and vomit, feeling like they'd seen into hell.

"Look in the DVD player," Denny managed to say, gesturing Harley inside. "But bring the whiskey first."

Harley ran, bringing back the bottle. "What's happened? Let me help. Let's get you both inside."

"No." Denny pushed him away. "You go and watch, but only for a minute. And turn the volume down."

Harley's hand stayed on Denny's back, eyes showing his confusion, but then he did as he'd been told, going inside.

A few minutes after Harley had gone Denny pulled the top off the bottle then took the longest draw he could manage, feeling it burn all the way down. He nudged at Richard's shoulder, prizing him up and pressing the bottle into his fingers. "Drink it. Probably not the best idea, but drink it anyway."

Richard did, his bloody hand shaking when he tried to grip the bottle. Denny wrapped his hands over the top and guided the way.

"I..." Richard tried but ran out of words immediately.

"Don't." Denny shook his head. "Nothing to say. Not yet." He wiped blood from Richard's cheek and took the bottle back. It slid in his grasp. Blood. Richard's blood, from his hand. He swallowed another enormous slug before passing it back.

Richard didn't even look at it, head back and throat working as soon as he got hold of it. Denny pulled him in, holding him tight while they passed the bottle back and forth until Harley returned. Then Richard turned away, face hidden against Denny.

Harley's face told its own story. He'd watched the DVD. Too much of it.

He stood over them and Denny could see the effort it was taking for Harley to keep himself under control. "Ritchie." His voice came out breathy, broken, as his hand brushed across Richard's head. Then he reined himself in even tighter, years' worth of fighting and discipline straightening his back. "I don't know what's going on, but I'll find out. There are some people on their way, some guys to secure the place plus a doctor." His gaze skittered back to Richard again but didn't linger, as though it were too hard to look.

"Do we need guards?" Denny asked.

"Don't know. Don't know if this is a threat or what it is. I—" Harley sucked in a huge breath. "I don't understand a fucking thing but I will."

Denny didn't doubt him for a second.

"You want me to help you get him inside and deal with his hands or do you want to wait for the doctor?"

"I can make it indoors on my own," Richard said, glancing up for the first time.

Now the rage was gone from his face, leaving only hopeless, utter despair that was even harder to look at. He leaned on Denny as he fought to stand. But between them they made it to their feet, the extra quantity of alcohol Richard had consumed making him rock. Denny strengthened his grip on Richard's shirt while he led the way back to the house. Richard held tight to the bottle.

Inside, Richard paused by the living room door, his gaze on the blank TV screen. Then he pushed himself forward, into the kitchen, collapsing on a chair. Harley found water and the first-aid kit when Denny lifted Richard's right hand in his. It was a mess, bloodied, with deep scratches, torn skin and wood splinters a mile long, all ripe for God knew what types of infection.

"Maybe we should wait for the doctor," Denny said, only too aware of the whiskey in his system and his own shaking hand.

"No." Richard looked at him briefly. "You do it." He swigged directly from the bottle again.

It was a long messy job, one that required several changes of water. Harley disappeared temporarily when a car loaded with men arrived, talking to them outside. Richard shook his head when the doctor came in and tried to take over, insisting that Denny continue to wash the wounds, pick out the splinters, press back ripped skin and bandage him up.

When Denny surveyed at his piss-poor effort, he thought that probably anyone could have done a better job. But no one would have wanted to do it as much as he did.

Richard was pretty nearly falling-down drunk by the time it was finished. The doctor tried to insist they eat something but all three shook their heads. Denny knew there wasn't a chance anything was going to stay down, not yet. Next the doctor tried to advise that sleep was the best thing, but Richard appeared flat out terrified at the prospect. When the doctor insisted, Richard started shouting, loud and angry, saying there was no way he could close his eyes, he knew what he was going to see. He pushed up from the table, staggering as he knocked things over, driving into Harley, eyes angry, mouth set hard, hands reaching for things to grab and break. Only, with the thick bandages, the best he could do was shove at them, sending them flying.

He would only go to sleep if the doctor could guarantee no dreams.

Denny, Harley and the doctor all looked at each other. Then the doctor produced a small bottle of pills, giving Richard two.

It took all three of them to practically carry Richard to bed and he was out, stone cold, a minute after his head hit the pillow. Denny climbed on next to him, his back against the headboard, his hand in Richard's hair. There was still blood on Richard's face, a spray from his hands, more from when he'd wiped at his eyes.

Harley passed a damp cloth without being asked, seemingly caught and lost by the state Richard was reduced to.

Denny washed Richard's face as gently as he could.

"Are you going to be all right?" Harley asked.

"Yeah." Denny carried on cleaning, soft strokes with his own bloodied hands.

"If I go, will you take care of him?"

Denny snapped his head up, feeling fiercely protective. "Of course I'll fucking take care of him. That's my job, not yours."

"I know, I know." Harley backed down immediately. "Just...try and keep him asleep. I want to have some answers for him by the time he wakes up."

"What's happening?" Denny asked, anger drained, attention back on Richard. "I thought Grady died in that old school building."

"So did I." Harley's voice started to crack. "He was my friend too, you know." Now there were tears. "I loved him too, and to die like..." He scrubbed at his face, hands way too harsh. "I don't understand but I'll find out. I promise you."

"I want you to make it go away," Denny admitted, tears dripping off his nose and falling onto Richard's cheek. "Make it go away like it never happened. But I know that's not possible. So settle it, Harley. I don't care how, but settle it."

"I will, if it's the last thing I do." Harley brushed away the last tears, standing up straighter. "I'm going to go but there'll be people here, you're safe. Nothing's going to get to you in here."

"It already has," Denny said quietly, but as Harley turned to go Denny called him back. "Where is it, the

DVD? I don't want it here, don't want Richard to see it again."

"I've got it." Harley touched his pocket lightly, as though it were poisoned. "I'm taking it to Detlef. He wanted it earlier but I need to be there when he sees it."

"Did you watch it all?" Denny looked up, eyes wide.

"No, but I'm going to."

"For God's sake, why? I've only seen the last couple of minutes but it was enough. Too much."

"I owe it to Grady," Harley said simply.

"I don't want to see it." Denny shook his head.

"You shouldn't. It's different for you. I was his friend. I'm about the past. You're Richard's future. You can't be stained by this. He needs you to get him through it."

"I will. I'll get him through." Denny's gaze went briefly to Richard, then back to Harley. "But we're all stained, the whole country. We're all stained with Grady's blood."

"Right now I want to spill everybody's," Harley said, and Denny could see in his eyes that he meant it. "I'm going to Detlef before that thought turns into a crusade." He stopped at the door, glancing back. "Get some sleep. You don't look so great yourself." And with that he was gone.

Only it wasn't as easy as that.

Denny curled around Richard, arm protectively across his chest, but when he closed his eyes, his head swam and he could see bright red blood. Grady's agonized face melted into Richard's, flesh became distorted, unreal, bodies bled and died. He opened his eyes as someone came to check on them, offering anything they needed. Denny waved him away. It was good to know people were there, that they were protected. But the house he'd come to think of as sanctuary, as home, had been invaded. It didn't feel like theirs anymore.

Richard woke at about four in the morning, desperately calling for Grady. Arms flailing wildly as he crashed about the room, incoherent and barely conscious. Denny watched until he pitched to the floor again, hands reaching out blindly when the tears started. He dragged Richard back to bed, cradling him between his splayed thighs as the doctor injected him with something certain to keep him asleep. Then he waited for the drug to take effect while Richard sobbed uncontrollably. Only when he was quiet again, hitched breathing warm against Denny's chest, did Denny look up to see Harley and Detlef in the doorway. Harley's face was racked by shock and horror. He'd seen the rest of the DVD all right. Detlef's face was closed up tight.

"Well?" Denny demanded.

"We've got things moving. All the information networks are running," Harley started to explain. "We're putting on pressure where we need to and—"

"Don't tell me what you don't know, tell me what you do."

Detlef moved forward slowly, perching on the edge of the bed. He rested a hand on Richard's ankle, gazing at the point where their skin met, the work-worn ridges of his fingers contrasting with the hair above Richard's sock.

"I remember when I first met Richard," he said quietly. "He was only about nineteen. A skinny little thing and skittish with it, pretty as a picture and scared as a rabbit caught in a headlight. Part of a stunning couple. Two pretty little boys who clung to each other desperately. The people around him were all talking about moral issues, the ethical and economic reasoning against slavery. All he was interested in was protecting Grady. One pretty boy standing guard over another. That never really changed, even when they both grew into men. And what men they were." He sighed.

"There was something about Grady, an aura, something. When you listened to him speak you'd follow him anywhere, do whatever he asked of you. Richard was different. He was quieter, less obvious, but there isn't a man anywhere I'd rather have watching my back or one whose opinion I value more." Detlef looked up at Denny. "They both deserved better than this. I let them down."

Denny didn't know the truth of that. He didn't know the truth of anything anymore. "What's happening? I don't understand."

"There was some explanation at the start of the DVD. Those men stood there, filming themselves, and told us what had happened and exactly what they were going to do." Now the signs of strain were starting to become evident, pinched lines around Detlef's mouth, a muscle twitching in his brow. "A lot of people had gathered in that old school building, ready to be moved to a new hiding place. Someone sold us out to the secret police – we've long since dealt with him. The police hit the place hard, most people got out. A lot of good ones died and we all thought Grady was one of them."

Detlef stroked over the protuberance of Richard's anklebone, smoothing out the line of his sock. His hand shook as he did it. "Obviously he didn't die. When they checked him he was still just about alive." He lifted his head, his eyes fixed on Denny's. "They nursed him back to health just so they could torture him to death. Why? Why would one human being do that to another? I can't..." He shook his head hard, turning away. "If you knew the answer to that there's no way you'd be here now, with Richard."

He sucked in a breath, businesslike again. "They were going to use the DVD against us somehow but we hit back. We destroyed some of their bases without even knowing they existed. Grady's death turned out to be the spur that brought about the end of the war and the DVD disappeared, God knows where."

"So why has it surfaced now?" Denny asked. "It came in this morning's mail. It was supposed to be from some little girls, a freedom song they'd made up and performed. They wanted to show Richard. I saw the letter, it's in the kitchen."

"I know. I've seen it as well. That was just a ploy to get him to watch it."

"Who sent it?"

"We don't know yet."

"Why now? What about the men in it? The ones who... What's happened to them? And whoever filmed it and has kept it all this time. What about all of them?" Denny needed answers.

"We don't know yet." Harley came and stood behind Detlef, his voice a vicious, hard snarl. "But we will and when we do they're going to pay. Pay with everything they have. You have my word on that. There's going to be blood and—"

Detlef stopped him with a hand on Harley's arm. "Enough. Denny doesn't want to hear what may happen. He wants to know what we've done." He looked back at Denny. "Truth is, not enough, but we will, trust me. Get some sleep now. Hopefully there'll be more news by morning. We're going to need you when Richard wakes up, so sleep until then."

Faith Ashlin

"I can't." Denny shook his head. "I keep seeing it. Him. If it's like this for me, what must it be like for Richard?" He stroked his hand through Richard's sweat-damp hair, his other one still fisted in the fabric of his clothes. He wasn't about to let go. He was never letting go.

"Then let the doctor give you something," Detlef tried again. "It doesn't have to be anything strong." He anticipated Denny's argument. "Something to take the edge off but will still let you wake up if you need to. It's either that or you'll be no use to us and him."

Eventually Denny agreed, taking the pill offered, and the nightmare stopped, just for a few hours. He slept fitfully, Richard pulled tight against him and a headache of truly epic proportions pounding at his skull.

He came awake the next morning when Richard began to stir by his side. One moment it was them, in their bed, warm and comfortable, the next it hit him again. The horror of Grady's face as he'd died. This wasn't going to go away. He reached instinctively for Richard, turning onto his side so they were face to face, a hand pressed to Richard's chest.

He watched as consciousness returned, emotions chasing themselves across Richard's features. The softness of sleep replaced by pain and loss and terror. Watching while Richard clamped down on it all, holding it tightly inside as he opened his eyes. Immediately Richard searched for him, easing back into the pillow a little when he saw Denny. Denny had never felt so glad for anything in his life. It was still the same Richard, still them, together.

"You look as bad as I feel," Richard said, his voice rough and dry as though it had been dragged over broken rocks.

"You look beautiful," Denny said. "How you doing?"

"Like shit. Like my head is full of cotton wool. What did they give me last night?"

"Don't know, but it worked. At least you got some sleep."

"Did you get any?"

"Yeah. The doctor gave me one of his magic pills."

"But you still watched me all night." It wasn't a question, more a statement of fact. "I..." Richard rubbed at his face. "I appreciate that."

"Hey, don't." Denny caught hold of his arm. "Don't appreciate it, expect it. That's what we do, you and me."

The tight grip Richard had on his emotions appeared to falter just for a moment, and he squeezed Denny's shoulder, hand brushing up against his neck. Then he reined himself in and sat up. "Do you know what's going on?"

"Detlef and Harley were here last night. They might still be. They said there was some explanation at the start of...the film, but I guess you already know that."

Richard's back stiffened but he nodded briefly. "Where is it? The DVD."

"Detlef has it." Denny wondered what Richard's reaction would be to that but there didn't seem to be any. "They said they might have more information this morning."

"Well, I suppose we ought to go find out." Richard stood up, offering a hand down to Denny.

It was that one simple gesture that almost broke Denny. Richard reaching for him, needing him. His throat tightened, his heart kicked against his chest and the next thing he knew he was up and hugging Richard hard.

Richard hugged back just as fiercely.

Then they went to face the rest of the world.

There was someone Denny vaguely remembered meeting before asleep on their sofa, another sprawled over an armchair, two more heading out of the back door. The kitchen looked more like a command center than his place of sanctuary. A couple of people nodded to them then made discreet exits. Stella Haynes was left sitting at the table.

She looked up, her face white as a sheet, eyes red and swollen, mouth rounding into an 'O' when she saw them. "I'm so sorry. I'm so very, very sorry." She half got up, dropped back down, then stood again, alternatively reaching for him and pulling her hand away. "That was the most... I don't know what... My God, I really am sorry, I..."

"Have you been crying?" Richard asked, his tone softer than Denny thought she deserved. "Haven't seen you cry in years. Not since you got your first decent dress and someone knocked you on your ass in the mud."

"Richard," she said. Then there were tears shining in her eyes.

In a heartbeat he pulled her in, holding her close and rocking her gently as she caught her breath. She was the one to pull away first, back under control, hand patting Richard's chest.

"Thanks, I... I'm—"

"Don't say you're sorry again," Richard said, not unkindly. "I know just what you mean."

"Okay." She sniffed and straightened her shoulders. "But I'm going to say sorry for being such an idiot before." She glanced at Denny then back to Richard. "You have a right to grab any bit of happiness you can get. You deserve it and I was a bitch for questioning you."

"You just admitted you were wrong. Fuck, Stella. Crying and admitting to a mistake? It's like a whole new world." Richard stroked her arm as she wiped at her face.

"I was a rotten friend, sorry." She turned to Denny. "I owe you an apology as well. I talked about you like you were… I was wrong to do that. I'm sorry."

Denny nodded, not sure how to take her, but Richard pulled her in for another brief hug. "Wow, but enough now, you're scaring me. It's like you've been taken over by body snatchers." Richard let her go. "Where is everyone?"

"Detlef asked me to call him when you woke up. We didn't know how long you'd be out for but he'll be here soon. Let me make you some breakfast while we wait."

"You want to cook? Fucking hell." Richard raised an eyebrow, like he would if things were normal.

"I can cook, I think. I'll do a big fried breakfast, get something solid inside you. You need it and that's what people do in situations like this. Even I can manage that and…" She was babbling and she looked like she knew she was.

"Don't bother." Richard stopped her with a hand on her shoulder. "I don't want anything. I'll grab a shower and try and make myself feel a bit more human before they get here."

"But you should have something. Please, let me do something." She was almost begging.

"Coffee," Richard said, and Denny marveled at the way he was still thinking of other people. "I could do with some good strong coffee."

Stella nodded. "Okay, and toast. I can make toast and it'll be good for you and…"

She was still talking to herself when they walked out of the room.

Chapter Eight

Detlef and Harley arrived as Denny was combing his damp hair and Richard was getting dressed. Richard hadn't shaved but Denny thought he looked better, a fraction anyway. He hoped it wasn't wishful thinking.

They all sat at the kitchen table drinking coffee, pushing around the toast Stella had made. Denny thought he should be hungry. All he'd had since throwing up yesterday was neat whiskey. But the thought of eating made his stomach muscles clench, and it seemed like Richard felt the same way.

Detlef went through all they'd already known then started on new information. A man, an old man from up in the mountains, someone they'd been aware of but long ago discounted, had been in possession of the film. He knew he couldn't stop them anymore, or bring down the movement. But he'd wanted to hurt them, hurt them all. Now he was sick, dying, and had decided it was time. He'd sent the DVD with all his hatred wrapped around it.

Harley said, voice quiet and hard, that the old man's time was now up. He'd been helped on his way. Richard simply nodded.

As for the rest, most of those in the film were already dead. There were two that the movement thought had been killed that might just possibly still be alive. They were going after them. There was nowhere they could hide, not after this.

Apart from that there really wasn't much else to be done. Grady had still been dead over five years. They still didn't know what had happened to his body, although they were trying on that. There was no one else for them to take revenge on. They sat around the table and looked at each other, lost.

"I want..." Richard started then stopped, biting at his lip. "I want to do something, go somewhere, hit something, break something. Kill someone. It doesn't feel right to just stay here. Are we supposed to carry on as normal?"

"I know exactly what you mean but I don't know what else we can do," Detlef admitted. "Don't we owe it to Grady to carry on trying to make things better?"

"I owe him more than that." Richard sucked in a harsh breath, pressing his eyes shut tightly for a moment. "I owe him... I owed him at least enough to go back and make sure he was really dead."

"Richard..." Voices all spoke at once, trying to reassure, but Richard ignored them all.

"I should never have just left him." He looked at Denny, face full of something Denny couldn't quite identify. "I won't make that mistake again."

"We all thought he was dead." Harley sounded as broken as Richard. "I saw him, I saw him get shot and go down. There was no way he could have survived—"

"But he did," Richard interrupted. "He was alive and I left him."

"It was me pulling you away." Harley's hands were shaking, his voice no better. "Me and Paulie and some of the others. You'd been hurt, there was blood pouring down your face, you could hardly see, you couldn't go."

"You were no better. Your leg was ripped open," Richard said, fingers digging into the surface of the table. "But I should have. I loved him. I'm Grady Porter's Richard after all."

"We all loved him," Stella said. "We all should have checked. I was closer than either of you, not hurt as badly, and there were others behind me. But we couldn't." Her gaze moved back and forth between Richard and Harley. "Grady was at the back, one of the last ones in the school building. The police were right on him. Nobody from his group made it out. Anyone who tried to get back there would have died. It would have been guaranteed suicide."

"I should have," Richard insisted.

"Listen to me." Detlef slapped a hand down firmly on the table. "I wasn't there that night but I've spent hours listening to what happened. By the time Grady was shot you couldn't have got to him, any of you. The police were on him practically before he hit the floor. He should have got moving earlier, but you know what he was like for checking and rechecking things."

"Don't you try and blame him for this," Richard snapped. "This is not Grady's fault, he didn't do anything wrong."

"Of course he didn't." Detlef's voice was just as loud, only much more controlled. "His double-checking saved us God knows how many times, but that time it cost him his life. It wasn't anybody's fault but the motherfucker who sold us out. He's the one to blame, Richard, not you. Him and the bastards that did that...monstrous thing to Grady. If he were still alive I'd do to him what they did to Grady, but he's not. You can't take this out on yourself instead."

Richard slumped back in his seat, a hand going up to rub at his mouth, the lines of his jaw set hard.

"Listen to Detlef," Denny said gently, reaching for Richard. "I never met Grady but from what I know of him, what I read and saw, what you've all told me, he wouldn't want you punishing yourself. You can't feel guilty about this. That's not how he'd see things and you have to do right by him."

"Do right by him?" Richard asked.

"Yeah, you're very much part of what he left behind, his legacy. You have to carry on for him. That means being strong, acting the way he'd want. Not letting those fuckers win."

Not letting them win. The words sat over all of them for a long moment. Denny thought that maybe being the one who hadn't been involved at the time meant he could see things most clearly. But where did they go from there?

They spent the rest of the day together, mostly because they didn't know what else to do. Time spent going over the same ground, thinking the same things, avoiding others. Detlef left early evening, leaving men guarding the gate although there was no discernible reason for it. They weren't under threat anymore, but... No one wanted to take them away.

They poured Stella into the backseat of a car very late that night, drunker than Denny had ever seen her, and watched as she was driven away. She'd hugged and kissed them all repeatedly, hanging onto

Richard's arm as tears threatened again. Tough old broad she might be, but Denny knew they were all in this together and Richard was as good as her family.

They carried on drinking until Harley practically passed out over the table. Carrying him between them they managed to get him on the sofa and Denny threw a blanket over him before heading to bed himself.

Richard was standing in the bedroom, staring out into the darkness through the window. Denny pressed a couple of pills into his hand and guided him into bed, trying to curl around him. But Richard didn't want that. Instead he rolled Denny onto his side, pushed up close behind him, threw an arm firmly around him, and pressed his mouth into Denny's hair.

Denny was woken just as dawn was breaking by Richard thrashing around, a nightmare clearly gripping him hard. With some effort he managed to wake him properly. Then he held him tight, until Richard inhaled sharply before getting up. Denny made a move to go with him but was gently pushed back.

"I'm all right now, honest. I'm just going to sit for a while and try and stop thinking. You go back to sleep. I need a bit of time on my own."

"You sure?"

"Yeah." Richard nodded, smoothing a hand over Denny's hair before pushing him gently back onto the bed.

When Denny woke later in the morning, Richard was still sitting at the kitchen table staring into nothing.

Detlef stopped by later that day, updating and checking on them. He stayed for a while, talking quietly around the hangovers. When he left, he asked with real concern, "Are you going to be all right?"

"Yeah." Richard nodded sharply. "I'll be okay."

But, Denny thought, it wasn't to be as simple as that.

Richard roamed around the house as though he didn't know what to do with himself. He drank too much, lashing out at things when he couldn't hold the anger in anymore. The television was the first casualty, ripped from the wall and thrown out of the window when Denny would have sworn Richard was already too wasted to even stand.

The outbuilding was practically destroyed on the fourth night, beaten and ripped at until Richard's hands were bleeding again. He stood in the middle of their land shouting at the moon or the sky, hands clenched into fists, chest heaving. Denny could do nothing but watch.

Richard didn't, couldn't, sleep without taking more pills than he should, plus half a bottle of whiskey. Then he'd crawl into bed when it was inky dark and curl around Denny, stroking at his hair or back with a heavy, uncoordinated hand. He'd whisper words that always included 'don't leave me' and 'I'll keep you safe.'

Denny wasn't going anywhere.

Eventually, Denny tried gentle hands and soft touches. He knew sex could be a good way to release pent-up feelings. If he could exhaust Richard through sex then he might stop hurting himself. Richard pushed him away until the night Denny insisted, hand against the hard ridge in Richard's jeans. At that point he was practically thrown across the bed, Richard's face red and set firm above him.

"Don't," Richard spat out. "I'll hurt you if we do it now and I can't do that."

"It's all right." Denny reached for him again. "I can take a bit of rough and you'd never really hurt me."

"No, don't you see? That's all I've got left." Richard's face started to crumple. "Not hurting you is all I've got." He pulled Denny close, burying his face in Denny's neck, breathing hard.

Denny only felt him crying when it was too dark to see.

With the darkness came the nightmares as well. Richard would scream out meaningless words, twisting and tangling himself in the sheets, drenched in sweat, waking with unseeing eyes and a face full of horror. It was then the radio or music was switched on, the volume turned up way too loud. Denny knew what that was about without Richard having to say a word.

Grady's screaming.

The sound had got into his head too, and at times, if he let himself remember it, he couldn't get it out. Screaming the likes of which he'd never heard before and prayed he'd never hear again, bouncing around in his mind. Yeah, he knew what the excessively loud music was for.

He tried taking Richard out but where was there to go? What could they possibly do? Instead he got Richard working on the land. The most physically demanding, back-breaking work he could think of just to tire him out enough to sleep. Richard went along willingly with everything he suggested.

After the first couple of days and a huge shouting match—which Denny won—Richard ate what he was given and drank when told. But he wouldn't give up the whiskey bottle no matter what Denny said. Nor did he seem like himself. It was as if his mind were elsewhere, focused on other things. Denny knew the truth of that.

They spent endless hours sitting shoulder to shoulder on the back step or outside in the sunshine, all while Richard would stare off into the middle distance as he told Denny all about Grady, talking until his throat was dry and raspy, telling stories from their younger days then older, good times and the not so good. When Denny eventually had to get up to make food, Richard would continue to sit, staring at nothing.

Two weeks in and Richard still looked like hell and they were all worried. Even Harley didn't want to get drunk with him anymore, pressing coffee into his hand, which Richard left around until it got cold. After three weeks, Denny didn't want to leave him alone, calling Harley if he had to go out.

One day Harley made Denny wait while he tried, hesitantly at first, to persuade Richard to get some professional help. This was a suggestion Denny had already put forward but Richard had dismissed it before the sentence was even fully out there. This time it came with Harley and Detlef's backing, but it made no difference. Richard wouldn't even think about it, even when Harley became insistent. It was only when tempers began to fray that Denny called a halt, adamant that they leave it for the day.

He'd try again later.

Of course, eventually, it hadn't been possible for Harley to come when he was needed and Denny had arrived back home from an important visit, late in the evening, to find Richard digging frantically and unnecessarily in the dark at the far edge of their land. He was shivering hard, cold to the bone, and wet down to his skin from the pouring rain.

Denny guided him back inside and maneuvered him into a hot shower. Then he got in with him, soaping up Richard's hair, running his hands over the cold, familiar flesh. After wrapping him in warm towels, they went back to the bedroom and Denny pressed him back onto the bed, hands again on his skin. This time he wasn't checking for new injuries or measuring weight loss. This was about connection and love.

He dropped a kiss on Richard's nipple, another on his collarbone, one to the base of his neck, a line along his jaw. A soft one to his lips. Richard didn't stop him. Emboldened, Denny pushed in with tongue and hips, something in his belly flipping when Richard's hand came up to brush over his hair. Denny kissed like he hadn't realized he knew how, trying desperately to say everything he wanted, things that words simply weren't enough for.

Richard kissed back, maybe not as hard nor with as much passion, but he kissed and that's what counted, right?

Hands stroking across flesh, Denny pushed Richard's thighs apart and slipped between them, pulling the towel out of the way. His mouth was on the line of Richard's full cock when Richard stretched down to cup his face, lifting him away. "You don't have to."

"Please." Denny rubbed his cheek against the tip. "Let me, I want to, I miss this. I miss the taste of you. Can I?"

Richard stayed silent, and when Denny looked up he was chewing at his bottom lip.

"I want this, for me," Denny tried again. "But you have to say yes. I can't just take."

After a long second Richard nodded while he drew patterns around and over Denny's ear.

Denny sucked the length into his mouth, his eyes falling closed as he reveled in the taste, the smell, the feel of it. He wanted this. Wanted.

Carefully, taking his time, he worked Richard with gentle hands and a less gentle mouth, lapping, licking, taking all he could get. He smoothed a hand out over Richard's hip, feeling bone and hard muscle, until he could curl his fingers around the curve of his ass, thumb pressing hard into flesh.

Lips sliding, mouth full, tongue pushing, lessons learned and remembered. This was it. This was home and where Denny wanted to be. Safe. With Richard to rely on, to lean against.

He bobbed his head down farther, wanting more, pushing Richard's thighs wider apart with the force of his shoulders, spreading and splaying them so he could burrow lower. More Richard. Surrounded by him, warm and solid and all man, as he smoothed his hands out over skin, capturing as much as possible.

He let Richard's cock slide deeper into his mouth and press toward the back of his throat, closing his eyes and drawing in breath through his nose. More, all, he wanted... Richard reached down to curl around his face, tracing the outline of his own cock through the skin of Denny's cheek before lifting, just a little.

Denny knew what that was all about. Taking Richard all the way down made his throat sore afterward and he didn't have permission for that. Didn't have permission to hurt himself.

He eased back, letting Richard's dick rub over the roof of his mouth, hollowing his cheeks, and felt Richard's breath hitch high and hard in his chest. He knew that as well. Knew that hitch and what it meant, and the realization of that knowledge made his belly flip again. This was his, where he belonged. He sucked once more, the right side of hard, and let his teeth glide against the length as he slid one hand back, pushing a knuckle under Richard's balls, sliding a fingertip closer. Not in, not now, just over and around, rubbing along tight muscle and... Richard's breath hitched again, his chest arching up.

Suck and slide, rub and ease back. Build the pressure, build it high until... He rubbed again, deliberately matching the timing with his mouth, and Richard came. Sighs of air, breathy gasps, mumbled versions of Denny's name, and Denny's throat was flooded.

He swallowed, difficult with a cock still deep in his mouth, but he wasn't ready to let go, not yet. Not ever. Above him Richard sighed again, sated, and his dick shifted, sliding out of Denny's mouth. Denny licked at his lips for the last of the taste, lapping along the shaft when it was all gone, nuzzling his nose into the coarse hair at the base. That earned him a lackadaisical snort of laughter and Richard's hand reaching down to grip his shoulder.

"Get up here," Richard said, pulling.

Denny went willingly, landing with a thump, half on, half off Richard.

"I needed that," Denny admitted, his nose millimeters from Richard's. "Needed you."

"The last few weeks have been hard on you, haven't they?" Richard cupped Denny's face, stroking slowly as he reached down with his other hand to find Denny's cock under the barely hanging on towel. He squeezed gently and Denny groaned, dark and breathy. "I've been a bastard to live with."

"No you haven't." Denny leaned in and, just as he'd hoped, Richard kissed him. A slow kiss full of familiarity and affection.

"Yeah, I have. You didn't sign up for that." He slid his hand again and Denny gasped into Richard's mouth.

"I did." Denny thrust up into his fist, hips working, back arching. "I signed up for all of you, for everything."

"I'm sorry." Richard worked him faster, harder, and Denny was already balanced on the edge, mouth pressed against Richard's cheek. "I'll be better from now on, I promise."

"You don't have to. It's hard. You..." Denny couldn't manage anymore as Richard tightened his grip, stroking again, and he came, belly shaking as his orgasm ripped through him.

"I promise," Richard whispered, easing him through the secondary shocks.

Denny smiled, small and satisfied when he buried his nose in Richard's neck, already fighting sleep. He slept long and more deeply than he had for many nights, his body finally relaxing completely. He was woken in the gray light of dawn by a crashing sound that had him up and out of bed in a heartbeat.

The stand that used to hold the television had been thrown through the newly glazed window in the living room. It had not only shattered the glass but also smashed the wooden frame holding it. Richard lay on the floor among the splinters, so drunk he was unconscious, covered in his own vomit.

Denny stood in the doorway and simply looked, weariness hitting him hard. He'd thought... He'd thought a lot of things but what did it matter? He'd seen enough of that DVD to know what it could do. It had been sent to hurt and it had worked. Grady had meant enough to him, in an iconic, detached way, but he hadn't loved him like Richard did. He could only imagine what must be going through Richard's mind. In the end he dragged Richard back to bed, washed him down, picked out the broken glass, cleaned his wounds and turned him on his side so he wouldn't drown in his own vomit if he threw up again.

What else could he do?

He climbed into bed next to Richard, steeling himself to wake every half hour to check on him.

Later that morning, Richard was still out cold but breathing deeply and steadily when Denny woke up. He left water by the bed and went to start his day. There was a window to patch, mess to clean up, and glaziers to phone before he could start work outside after all.

By midmorning, he was just about to head back to the house to check on Richard yet again when he saw him sitting on the back step, watching. Denny stuck his spade into the dirt, exhaled slowly, and walked resignedly over.

"How you feeling?" he asked, standing over Richard.

"Honestly?" Richard glanced up, squinting against the sun. "Like shit. But it's my own fault."

"Drink some water, a lot of it. It'll make you feel better."

"I think it's going to take more than water to do that." Richard rubbed a hand over his face. "I'm sorry, man. I'm sorry for being such an asshole and not being able to get past this. I'll understand if you've had enough, if you want to take off. You shouldn't have to put up with my crap."

Denny shifted his feet, folding his arms across his chest then purposely uncrossing them again. "I told you last night I'm here because I want to be, because I love you. I mean it and I'm staying. But this has to stop. It has to. Not for my sake but for yours, you can't carry on like this. You're going to end up dead or insane and I can't accept either of those options."

Richard chewed at his lip, then his finger, biting until there were traces of blood. "It's the screaming." He bit some more, harder. "I can hear him screaming. Most of the time I can block it out, but when it's dark and quiet, it's there and I can't stop it. I hear him screaming and it won't stop. I remember that sound from when I was young and my dad was... It's like a repeat of my worst nightmare. Only it's actually worse now and I still can't do anything to stop it."

Crouching down in front of him, Denny rested a hand on each of Richard's knees. "Then why don't you try what Harley suggested and get some professional help? It's not a sign of weakness or disloyalty to Grady."

Richard looked up at that, his gaze sharp on Denny's face.

"I know how your mind works," Denny went on. "You think that because you loved him, that he was your partner, you should be able to handle this and you're letting him down if you can't. But you're not, you're really not. This is way too much for anyone to deal with."

"It's like he died twice." Richard's face twisted with pain. "And if I thought the first time was bad, this is —"

"I know. I can imagine." Denny rubbed a hand along Richard's thigh. "But you can't go on like this because you're destroying yourself. I'll do all I can to help but you have to make a decision, right here, right now, to do something. This can't go on."

Richard opened his mouth to speak but no words came. There really was nothing left to say. His face looked so desolate that it told its own story. Denny curled a hand around the back of Richard's neck and pulled him closer, resting their foreheads together.

* * * *

Maybe, just maybe, things did improve after that.

Richard sat on the back step for a long time after they'd talked, watching Denny as he worked. He sat, obviously thinking.

Denny knew how his mind would be working. Things couldn't go on as they had been because he was hurting Denny and that couldn't be tolerated. He'd let down one man, watched him suffer. He wasn't going to do it again.

If that's what it took to make Richard change, then Denny would push that thought as hard as he had to.

He watched as Richard dragged himself up and went inside to shower. Then he shaved for the first time in days and changed the bed sheets after he'd dressed. He even made lunch, and Denny watched again as Richard forced himself to eat it and act normally.

Four days later and Denny was starting to think that perhaps the very worst was over. He wasn't foolish enough to think there wouldn't be setbacks when the world would look as bad as it had that first day. But perhaps there wouldn't be as many or they wouldn't be as bad?

All he could do was hope and watch.

He could see Richard making a real, sustained effort. He knowingly put the whiskey bottle down, made himself go to bed at a reasonable hour—even if he did still need the pills to actually sleep. He worked hard all day on the land but he wasn't just doing what

Denny told him anymore. He was thinking, deciding and anticipating what needed to be done next.

Denny felt a little surge of hope grow in his belly. They could get through this, they would.

Harley came around, looking pleased if drained, and suggested they go out for a drink. Maybe the bar was one step too far—Richard couldn't handle all the concerned faces, not yet—but he would, sooner rather than later, he said. They went shopping instead, to the supermarket of all places. But it was good to be pushing the cart with the wonky wheel around, arguing over breakfast cereals.

Richard was on more of an even keel and Denny felt the gnawing anxiety ease just a little.

After another couple of days Harley slapped Denny on the back and told him what a good job he'd done. How they couldn't have helped Richard without him. Denny knew it wasn't over yet, that Harley was way too soon with his congratulations. He'd seen Richard sitting, staring into space, mind obviously elsewhere. Worse, he'd watched the involuntary shudders cross Richard's face when unwanted images had reared back up. Watched him fight them back down, trying to ground himself in work and normality.

This hadn't gone. This was something that would live with them all forever, but maybe it was a start. He thought so. He even began to let Richard go out on his own.

Let Richard… Now there was a thought. Since when did he 'let' Richard do anything?

Since the sky had fallen in.

But maybe they were starting to fix that. It might involve Richard making an effort all the time but it was working and he did smile. Sometimes.

* * * *

Denny got out of the shower after another long day of working and wrapped the towel around his waist. He hated to admit it but he'd missed Richard being with him that afternoon, and it wasn't just for the company. He'd missed the help, having to do all the strenuous labor himself. He'd gotten used to Richard helping and now the muscles in his arms ached like hell. But Richard had needed to go into town. There were bank managers and lawyers to see. Denny was pretty sure it wasn't a way of getting out of working. Pretty sure.

He liked the thought even if it meant he was wrong.

He slung on an old T-shirt and sweatpants then wandered out to the kitchen only to find that... Holy shit, Richard had cooked dinner, real food that didn't come out of the freezer and go in the microwave.

"Wow, this looks amazing," he said, staring at the properly laid table. No mess, no piles of junk. It hadn't been like this for weeks.

"I thought we could have something really nice." Richard smiled, almost shyly. "Not that what you cook isn't nice. It's just that I haven't really been appreciating it."

"I get it." Denny smiled back. "What can I do to help?"

"Nothing. Sit, it's all ready."

It was all ready, good food, served well. "Did you really do all this?" Denny asked.

"Well." Richard scrunched his nose up. "With a little help from the restaurant on Brook Street."

"You fucking cheat." Denny laughed. "You had me going there."

"It's supposed to be the thought that counts."

"It is," Denny agreed. "This is really nice, thanks." He reached for the wine.

"You're welcome, but go easy on the booze," Richard said, his voice going dark. "I have plans for after."

When dessert was finished, Richard led the way to the bedroom, kissing Denny softly and deeply as they undressed, long, lingering kisses with way too much tongue to simply be hot. This was so much more. Intense, but also slow — thoughtful even — and with so much affection in every kiss that Denny thought his toes might just possibly curl.

Unexpected in the extreme, but Denny decided that, for once, he wasn't going to question everything. He was going to lie back and enjoy whatever he was lucky enough to get.

Richard pressed him onto the bed, hand gentle on his chest, mouth still ghosting over his lips as he pushed and arranged limbs to his own design. Then Richard touched him in a way he never had before, exploring every millimeter of skin, stroking, tasting, mapping every muscle, every plane and ridge, every hair follicle and pore from the very top of his head to the soles of Denny's feet and back again.

Touched Denny in the same way Denny had done to him, right back at the beginning. Richard had never been able to copy it before, but now Denny could feel the love that infused every touch, every taste.

All this from the man who had found it so difficult to touch.

Carefully placed kisses that drove Denny slowly, deliberately crazy. Crazy not from lust or sex or the physical reaction, although, if he had been thinking straight, he'd have to admit that was pretty spectacular. No, it was the way Richard did it, hands smooth and gliding, brow creased in concentration, like he had to do this properly. Had to get it right.

The way every brush of fingertip or tongue was filled with so much love that Denny wanted to melt under it.

"Ritchie?" Denny breathed, trying to twist his head around so he could see over his shoulder.

"Shh." Richard placed a kiss to the small of Denny's back, hands sliding down over his hips. "I want to know you, all of you. I want to show you, want you to know."

"Know what?" Denny arched, back taut as a bow string when Richard's tongue ran down the length of his spine.

"What you mean to me." Richard pressed his face to the top of one rounded cheek, his palms spread wide, high over Denny's shoulder blades, thumbs pushing into the tight cords of his neck, sliding down. "What you've done for me." Hot breath on hard muscle, teeth nipping sharply on his hip. Hands curled over his sides, fingers firm. "How much I appreciate it." Hands pulled him open. "And how much I love you." Opening him, licking and lapping down the gap, lips pressed firmly against him, tongue pushing in.

"Ritchie." Denny couldn't stop himself from rearing up, grabbing at the wooden spindles of the headboard, voice a desperate, breathy roar.

"Shh." Richard breathed the sound into him, hands rubbing and stroking between Denny's legs, over, under and around his balls. "I want this, need it."

The intent behind those words made Denny's belly clench tighter than any touch ever would.

Richard eased in again, his hands lifting Denny's hips, splaying his thighs wider so he could get in closer. Thumbs held him open, fingertips claiming, tongue deep.

Denny mewled, the sound small and feeble as he stretched his neck back, giving in to every sensation like he never had before. It had been ingrained in him when he was very young that you never, ever really let yourself go. Always hold something back, keep something for yourself that was safe and hidden from the world. It was the slave's golden rule. The only way to survive with a part of yourself left intact.

But now his mantra was "Richard, Richard, Richard." All he wanted, all he could feel was Richard. He'd never felt more right about anything in his life. Richard could have – did have – all of him and he was glad to give it.

"Now." Richard shoved in one last time with tongue and mouth. "Now I want to fuck you. I want to slide in so deep that you'll feel me in your belly, that all of you'll be mine."

Again Denny made that pathetic sound, muscles straining back, craving anything Richard would give him. Desperate to offer himself even further.

"But you're not going to come, not yet." Richard pulled himself up to his knees, pushing and playing with the relaxed muscle, dipping in and teasing. "I want you to do that after, in my mouth, so I can taste you." He lined himself up, hands holding Denny's hips, easing in slowly and thoroughly on one continuous glide. "And then" – he huffed, catching his breath – "I'm going to do this all over again until you're so hard it hurts and you're begging me to fuck you. I want this to go on all night."

Richard got what he wanted as Denny gave himself until there was nothing left to give.

* * * *

Stretch and elongate. Denny arched his back as hard as he could and felt the muscles pop. He grinned, catlike and satisfied. He ached—or rather, his ass did—and it was glorious. His world was good this morning, damned good.

Okay, so he wasn't stupid. They still had their problems. But the sun was streaming in through the curtains and the bed was soft. He felt like he'd been well and truly fucked last night, fucked so good that his body was still saying a lazy 'yes'. Plus, Richard was curled up asleep with his nose pressed against Denny's shoulder and a possessive hand on his belly. Did life get much better than that?

Richard opened one eye and smiled. "Hi." Denny knew that tone, knew it meant Richard was ready for more.

Yeah, life got better. The only cloud on the horizon was the fact that he had an appointment at the bank in—he twisted around to look at the clock on the bedside table—an hour. Plenty of time. Why had Richard made it so early anyway? *Don't waste time wondering about that.* There were much, much better things to do.

He scooted over, nose to nose with Richard, and kissed him sweetly and wetly, just the way that made Richard laugh. It worked, like Denny knew it would.

Richard wiped across his mouth with the back of his hand when he came up for air, grinning madly. "You do that on purpose, don't you?"

"Who, me?" Denny leaned in for another wet kiss. "I can't help it if I have a lot of saliva."

"Lying bastard."

Denny caught hold of Richard's shoulders and rolled them both until he was flat on his back, Richard securely on top. He kissed him again and again, more urgently now, conscious of the time. Richard gave back as good as he got, pliant as Denny adjusted him, pulling his legs down on either side of his own, reaching his hand down or around or...goddamn it, how was he meant to get to Richard's ass? He maneuvered again, ever thankful for his long arms as he slipped a lube-coated finger inside and Richard grinned against his mouth. "Someone's in a rush."

"I'm a busy guy. Got places to go, people to see," Denny said.

Richard pushed down on the finger, catching his lip between his teeth as he did so.

Denny sighed in pleasure at the sight. "It's your fault. You made the appointment."

"I'm not complaining." Richard let the words float out and Denny eased in a second finger, working him perfectly.

"Neither am I." He pressed up, watching Richard's face. Like a fucking oil painting. Who needed porn when you could watch Richard's face as he was being fingered open?

"This what you want?" Richard asked, eyes shining like they used to.

"Yeah, do you mind?" Denny curled his hand around Richard's hips, moving him up and down as he added a third finger.

"Mind? Me? No," Richard said quietly. "You can have whatever you want."

"Whatever?"

"Yeah." Richard pressed down, arching back into Denny's hand, eyes closing briefly.

"Then I want to watch your face while I fuck you like this." He pulled his fingers free, lifting Richard easily and flipping them over so he could loom above him. "Ready?" He slicked his cock and lined himself up.

"Oh yes." Richard grinned, easing his legs back, offering himself.

Denny slid home, that was the only word for it, exhaling nosily as he went. Fuck, that was good. Richard's body seemed to curl and press around him, dragging him in, holding him there, and Denny couldn't see a reason to ever leave.

But this wasn't going to last long, and it had nothing to do with the time.

Long thrusts pushed Richard up the mattress and made Denny shake and shiver way too soon. Moans and groans, the sound of flesh on flesh, the smell of Richard in his nose, the feel of skin under his hands, watching Richard's face as he arched and pressed back, meeting Denny every step of the way all combined to be too good, too much, too downright fucking impossibly perfect.

Denny came with Richard's cock in his hand, Richard's juice splattering over their bellies, reaching for Richard's mouth with his own.

A quickie in the very best sense of the word. Fucking perfect.

With a groan that had nothing to do with pleasure, Denny rolled out of Richard and off the bed. Standing up and stretching, he yawned. "Don't want to get up. Want to spend the whole day in bed with you."

"You want to sleep." Richard lay back and grinned. "Lazy ass."

"Want to do that as well. But not all the time." Denny stroked a hand over Richard's ankle. "I'm going to get a shower, though, seeing as some of us have a reason to get up."

Richard was still in bed when Denny got back and started dressing. He sat propped up against the headboard, hands behind his head, and watched, face curiously clouded.

"What do you want for dinner tonight?" Denny asked. "I could pick something up on my way back."

"Whatever." Richard shrugged.

Denny found his last elusive shoe and stood ready to go. "Okay. I should be back by lunchtime. Can you make a start on that patch of ground by the west corner? It needs digging over and feed mixed in." He stopped, grinning. It felt good to be talking about normal, ordinary things again. He hadn't realized he had such a craving for the ordinary. "I'll make it worth your while." He dropped a kiss on Richard's lips then headed for the door.

"Hey," Richard called out.

"What?"

"Nothing." Richard's smile was small, curling at his lips. "Just remember, I love you."

"Soppy bastard." Denny laughed. "You said it last night. I believe you."

"I hope you do," Richard said quietly.

"And I love you, you idiot," Denny yelled from halfway along the hallway. Then the door banged and he was gone.

* * * *

The trouble with the bank was there was nowhere to park, Denny thought, screwing his face up in annoyance as he circled the block. All right, so normally there was but today was Tuesday, which meant market day, which meant hundreds of moms with their shopping bags, kids, and their stupid huge cars. All so they could buy so-called fresh fruit and vegetables that were probably rejects from the supermarkets anyway. That and tacky clothes they only got because they were cheap. They'd never wear them. He scowled again, circling for what felt like the nine millionth time and...

A space. He shot forward into it. Thank fuck for that otherwise he'd be here all day. It was stupid, having to come this morning. Why couldn't he have gone with Richard yesterday? It wasn't like either of them were doing anything secret or important. He was only setting up a business account and Richard had to countersign it anyway. Him, ex-slave Denny, having a 'business account'. He couldn't help but smile at the thought as he pulled the key from the ignition.

Why hadn't he come with Richard yesterday?

Why had Richard made him a separate appointment today?

Why had he said 'I love you' like that when Denny was leaving?

And last night?

Denny thrust the key back in, gunned the engine and reversed out with no regard to anything behind him. He hit the road going as fast as his old truck would manage.

Back at the house everything looked exactly like he'd left it. Was that hammering in his chest just him being pathetic? The sight of Richard's car parked out the front made him feel a little foolish. The back door was still open, the radio was still on in the kitchen. Okay, so maybe there was no one out working on the land but perhaps Richard simply hadn't managed to drag his fine ass out of bed yet.

Denny found himself running into the kitchen. Empty. "Richard," he called.

Living room. Still a mess, but empty.

"Ritchie," he yelled, the muscles in his stomach contracting.

Bedroom, bed unmade, looking warm and inviting but empty.

"Richard," he shouted, the sound ripping at his throat.

Bathroom, only place left, but there was no sound of running water and the door wasn't locked and...

Richard was sitting on the floor, his back against the bathtub, eyes closed, lashes dark against his pale face. His chest was scarcely rising and falling as his hands rested on his thighs. The blood from his slashed wrists had soaked into the white of his T-shirt and the gray cotton of his sweatpants. An old-fashioned cut-throat razor lay on the tiles next to him.

Chapter Nine

"Ritchie." The single word escaped Denny's lips as he dropped to his knees at Richard's side. "What have you done?"

But it was pretty damned obvious what Richard had done, what the result would be if Denny didn't do something about it right now. Richard was alive. He had to be.

And Denny was going to keep him that way.

"You fucking stupid bastard." Gone was the whispered disbelief at his first sight of Richard. Now he was all single-minded action.

He pulled a shirt from the back of the door, wrapping it as tightly as he could around one of Richard's wrists and squeezed hard. There were three long cuts down his left arm, jagged but precise. Richard had known what he was doing. He'd meant business when he'd made those cuts. Denny tried to ignore them as he held the flesh together.

He grabbed Richard's other hand but he wasn't about to let go of the first, not yet. He pushed that under his leg, sitting back on his heels to press down with all his weight. Richard slid sideways, his eyes staying shut, his breath just puffing past his lips, only held upright by the points where Denny had him pinned.

Denny twisted the second wrist in a towel. It was too thick, too bulky—it wouldn't do the job right. He pressed it into the floor with one hand, searching in his jeans pocket for his cell phone. It clattered out, falling to the tiles with a loud crack. It had to still work, fucking had to. His hand slithered over the keys, wet with...

Wet with Richard's blood.

Don't think about that. Don't think about Richard's blood or anyone else's. Don't think about the warm sticky feel, thicker than water, so much more vital and a smell like no other. One that got in your nose and clouded your brain.

Don't think about any of it. Not Richard's life literally running through your fingers.

He couldn't hit the keys, not accurately, not with his left hand. But he needed his right, needed it to keep up the pressure through the damned not-tight-enough towel. He hit the second speed dial knowing the first was Richard and the second...

"Harley, get a fucking ambulance over here. Now." Then he squeezed on Richard's wrists again and prayed to a God he didn't believe in that he was in time.

* * * *

The next hour or so was a blur of practical, no-nonsense activity that had Denny wanting to shout louder than he ever had before. Keep Richard alive until the ambulance arrived. Hand over responsibility to the paramedics. No, that was one thing he couldn't do. It didn't matter if he knew he was getting in the way. They'd made it this far because they'd done it together. He wasn't backing out now and no one was taking Richard from him.

He'd never had anything his entire life and now he did. Now he had something more important than anything he ever thought possible. Fuck the paramedics, fuck the world—he was keeping what was his. No one was taking Richard from him, and that included Richard himself.

He sat way too close in the ambulance, walked as near as he could get as Richard was wheeled through the hospital and taken to a special treatment room. He was expected, that was clear. Harley, Detlef and some others stood by the door. The medical personnel were inside, gloved and ready to go.

This was Grady Porter's Richard and they were going to work miracles for him.

But it was Denny who would keep him alive. Denny, the filthy ex-slave that Richard had bought a little over a year ago. Denny, who'd never had anything so never learned how to want, but he wanted, needed Richard now.

Heavy wooden doors closed behind Richard as the doctors went to work. Denny stayed pressed close to the glass window, watching. Harley, then Detlef, tried to talk to him but he couldn't hear them and brushed their comforting hands away. His future was laid out on the table inside.

Richard was so pale, so very pale, freckles standing out like shadowy splatters of mud against too-white skin. Dark smudges around his eyes looked like bruises. Lips were drained of color, a foot fell limply to the side. Frantic activity was all around him. A basin was held out, material dropped into it, dark, dark, dark with drying blood. Richard's blood.

The shock hit Denny like a punch to the gut. It was his shirt. He'd used the shirt he'd bought himself only last week to bind Richard's wrist, and now it lay in a plastic container in a hospital, soaked with Richard's blood. He had no idea why but that hurt more than anything had a right to.

For a moment the doctor moved, clearing his line of sight, and Denny could see Richard's hand. It rested palm up while they worked on his wrist, fingers curled slightly upwards and in. Fingers that only hours earlier had been stroking through his hair as they'd moved together in bed.

Denny pressed his hand firmly over his mouth to stop himself from making a sound.

People passed behind him but he took no notice. Someone was talking to Harley, whispered words, glances in his direction. Denny ignored it all. If he weren't careful he'd start screaming and never stop.

Screaming.

It seemed to be a theme in his life lately.

Harley came and stood near him, shoulder just lightly brushing his. "Denny," Harley said. No 'Tassel Boy' now. "Why don't you put this on?" He held out a sweatshirt.

What? Why? Denny wasn't cold. At least he didn't think he was and... He looked down at himself. His light blue shirt was covered with stark patches of dark color. Richard's blood. He sucked in a breath and held himself tight, shaking his head at Harley. What did it matter? What did any of it matter?

"Please, man." Harley pushed the sweatshirt at him again. "You're scaring everyone. Fuck it, you're scaring me. I mean, that's a lot of blood. Can anyone survive after…?" His voice started to crack and he clammed up tight.

Denny grabbed the shirt, shucking out of his own and putting it on without taking his attention from the glass of the connecting door. He took one last look at his blood-stained shirt before throwing it into a corner. It was gone a minute later.

He was still standing there, nose almost pressed against the smooth surface, when the doctors came out to talk to them. They looked to Detlef first, then Harley, Denny forgotten as unimportant. Harley kept the group close so they could all hear as the doctors explained. Richard was going to be all right. He'd lost a significant amount of blood, the cuts on his right wrist, made with his left hand, were rough and deep. They'd needed careful stitching. The wounds on his left wrist were more clinical and would heal better. He'd been given something to make him sleep and shouldn't wake for a few hours. Then they'd see about a psychiatric evaluation and…

Denny didn't hear much of it past the fact that Richard was going to be all right.

He'd deal with the rest later.

The doctor said they could go in to see Richard while a room was made ready for him. As usual Detlef took control of the situation, striding forward. It was Harley that caught his arm, nodding to Denny, who'd been left standing in the corridor. They stepped aside as Denny went in alone.

He stood by Richard's head, looking at his face. Although he was horribly white, he looked peaceful, as though he were simply asleep and dreaming with dark lashes against pale skin, no sign of the turmoil that had driven them here.

Harley and Detlef came in, talking softly, touching Richard's hand, his forehead, almost as though they wanted to check he was actually still alive.

Detlef turned, asking Denny a question, but he still wasn't listening. He pushed by them, reaching in to wipe a trace of blood from Richard's cheek with his thumb. He remembered doing something like that before, cleaning blood from Richard's face. He didn't want to do it ever again.

"I thought he was doing better," he whispered, the first time he'd said anything for what seemed like hours.

"But you knew, when it mattered." Harley stood close to him, his face a mask of his own pain and failure. "You knew when he had me fooled. I would have gone to the bank, had I been you. But you..." He squeezed Denny's shoulder. "You went back. You're the only reason he's still alive."

Denny didn't know if that was true or not but it was good to hear.

A while later Richard was moved to a small secluded room on his own. The blinds were closed and he was settled down for the night.

Harley hovered by the end of the bed. "Do you want a lift home?" he asked eventually.

Denny shook his head as he went to sit in the high-backed chair in the corner. "I'm not going anywhere."

"But... Okay." Harley nodded. "I'll stay with you. I'll go and find us something to eat and —"

"No." Denny cut him off. "You go. I don't need anyone here."

Harley chewed at his lip and it caught Denny's attention in an abstract kind of way. He'd never seen Harley indecisive before. He was always the clear-thinking, resolute man of action. Now he'd been reduced to Denny telling him what to do.

"Go home," Denny said, turning away from him to look at the bed. "You can come back in the morning."

Quietly, without argument, Harley did as he was told, taking Detlef with him.

Richard didn't wake during the night, sleeping through the frequent medical checks. Denny caught a few hours of sleep, broken into small bits, woken by the constant need to check on Richard. He watched the rise and fall of Richard's chest while he slept, waiting for his eyes to open.

It happened eventually, about five in the morning as a nurse was stretching over him, inspecting something. Richard flailed around in the bed for a moment, confused and disoriented, until Denny caught his hand. Richard's gaze fixed on Denny's face then, his breath coming in sharp, ragged puffs.

"It's all right," Denny reassured him, repeating the words until the nurse finished her examination and left them alone. Then Denny traced a hand across Richard's cheek, rearranging his mussed hair. "You didn't expect to wake up, did you?"

"Denny…" Richard's voice was a ravaged, scratchy hiss. "I…"

"Shh." Denny patted him. "Go back to sleep. The nurse said you'll feel dazed for a while. Sleep. Let the doctors look you over again. I'll still be here when you wake up. We can talk then."

Richard fell back to sleep, his fingers twisted painfully with Denny's.

* * * *

When Harley and Detlef arrived at the hospital, there was a group of people in Richard's room. Denny was still sitting in the chair by the wall, an array of medical staff arranged around the bed. Richard was propped up by a pile of pillows, the white of his heavily bandaged arms stark against the covers. It seemed like a whole heap of tough talking was happening.

"What's going on?" Detlef wanted to know.

Everyone turned to look at him but even the senior doctors hesitated in front of the great man. Denny decided to fill the void.

He summed up the situation succinctly. "Richard's woken up again. The doctors have checked him over and declared him physically okay. Now they want him to talk to a head doctor, which he damned well should do. Only, because he's a stubborn son of a bitch, he's refusing."

Richard looked from Denny to Detlef. "I don't need a psychiatrist. I'm not crazy."

"No, just suicidal," Denny deadpanned.

"Your friend is right," one of the doctors spoke up. "You need to talk to someone professionally. We can help you and..." The whole shebang was about to start up again.

"Wait." Detlef held up a hand. "Richard, you're going to have to talk to someone, if only to shut me up, but..." He carried on right over Richard's protest. "Maybe it doesn't have to be right now." He glanced over at the doctors, checking. "We can give you a day or two to recover, to talk you into it. What do you say?"

"I'm not talking to a psychiatrist." Richard went to fold his arms across his chest but stopped as soon as he moved them.

"We'll talk him into it," Detlef assured the doctors, sounding confident in his own ability. They seemed confident enough as well, confident enough to leave shortly after. Detlef pulled up a chair and Harley perched on the foot of the bed.

"Have you had something to eat? You need anything?" Harley stuck to the practical.

Detlef cut straight to the chase. "You're a stupid bastard. You scared the shit out of us all."

Richard studied them both and didn't say a word, his face rigid.

"Maybe we could all use something to drink," Detlef tried again, softer this time. "Let's get something hot before we talk. What do you want, coffee?" He stood up and moved toward the door. "I'll go and get it. Denny, how about you?"

Denny looked at the obstinate figure in the bed and his lips thinned to a tight line. "I want you to leave now," he said abruptly to Harley and Detlef. It was most definitely an instruction, not a request. "I need to talk to Richard."

"It's all right. We're here to help." Detlef laid a reassuring hand on Denny's arm. "We'll all talk to him."

"No." Denny twisted until the hand fell away. "This is between the two of us. You need to leave."

Detlef appeared bemused. No one questioned him, let alone told him what to do.

"Come on," Harley said quietly, already reaching for the door. "Let them have a bit of space."

"But our place is with Richard," Detlef said, brow furrowing. "We can't just leave him."

"Yeah?" Harley's face went hard and his hand had a tiny shake in it. "Where were we when Ritchie was falling down drunk in his own puke? Or when he wouldn't, couldn't sleep, pacing around for hours? When he had nightmares so bad he had to smash things up to stop the noises and images playing over and over in his head? When he cried or hurt himself? When he was dying in front of our eyes? Where were we then?" His gaze went to Denny in a silent plea for understanding or forgiveness or something, not even acknowledging the man in the bed. "We left it all to Denny because we couldn't face our own guilt." He exhaled hard, running a hand over his face. "Give the kid a break. Let him try because if he can't do something with Richard then we're well and truly fucked."

"But I..." Now Detlef was left without words as he stared between them.

"Let's go," Harley said, holding the door open.

"I can't," Detlef admitted. "I can't just leave."

"Then we'll wait outside and run to Denny's rescue if he needs us." He ushered Detlef out, turning back to look at Richard. "I love you, man," he said simply before giving Denny a tight nod.

Then it was just Richard and Denny left in the room.

Richard glanced over at Denny. They hadn't really spoken since he'd woken up again. First there'd been nurses, then doctors, then more doctors with their arguments and concerned eyes. Now it was just them. "Are you going to come over here and be nice to me?" Richard asked.

"No." Denny shook his head slowly. "Because, right now, I'm so angry that if I touch you I'm likely to punch you in the face."

That made Richard's eyes open wide in surprise.

"You planned it all, didn't you? Careful, almost military planning, like during the war." Denny's voice was low and hard. "You must have gone out and bought that razor, hidden it away from me. Arranged my appointment at the bank to make sure I was out of the way. But that was nothing compared to what came before, the long-term planning to make me think you were doing better. Because that's what it was, wasn't it? It was all an elaborate act so I'd be fooled into leaving you alone. You played me for a right sucker. This was no spur-of-the-moment, overcome-by-despair act. This was you making a plan and carrying it out."

"I'm sorry." Richard's voice trembled just a little.

"Sorry's not good enough." Denny glared. "It doesn't even begin to cover it."

"I..." Richard dropped his head. "I don't know what else to say. I mean it. I'm sorry for hurting you and for you having to find me and..."

"Is that it? Is that all you're sorry for?"

"No. Yes, I..." Richard stumbled over the reply as though he didn't know how to answer.

"And the other night, what was that? A goodbye fuck? Something for me to remember you by?"

"No. I didn't mean it like that."

"So how did you mean it?" Now the anger was thick in Denny's tone.

"If anything, it was for me to remember you by." Richard's look never left Denny's face. Bewilderment colored his expression.

"But you weren't going to remember anything, were you? You were going to be dead, you fucker." Denny ran a hand over his eyes much too hard. His face felt twisted and tense, his body much the same. "Because if I didn't know you as well as I do, you wouldn't be here. You'd be cold and laid out in the morgue."

"I'm sorry," Richard said again, voice suddenly gone small. There was blood on the back of his hand. Dried blood. His blood.

"Stop saying that. Because it doesn't count for anything if you don't mean it and you don't. Otherwise you'd never have done it."

"I'm sorry for hurting you and I do mean that." He sounded like he truly did.

"I'm such an idiot." Denny shook his head again. "I believed in you, I really did. I believed you wouldn't lie to me."

"But I didn't. I never lied."

"Oh, don't give me that crap." Denny got up, pacing across the room to stand over the bed. "You promised me. You sat in the kitchen, in front of everyone, right after we saw that DVD, and promised. You promised me that you wouldn't leave me. How did you say it? Oh, yeah. 'I should never have just left him.' Grady. 'I won't make that mistake again.' That meant me." Now Denny was shouting, his voice full of fury. "You said you'd never leave me and then you fucking plan how you're going to trick me so you can ditch me with nothing."

"It wasn't nothing. I wouldn't do that." Richard seemed to be fighting to keep up. "I made sure you were taken care of. You'd get the house, the car, any money I have, everything."

"You planned that as well?"

"I saw a lawyer and—"

"I don't want your fucking house or money," Denny yelled down at Richard. "I don't want any of it. Is that what you think I'm after? Is that how little you know me? Jesus shit, don't you get it? Don't you get any of it? I want you. I want you to love me."

"But I do..."

"I want to trust you. I want you to mean it when you say you won't leave me. I want a fucking future."

"But I can't do it." Now Richard was shouting back. "I tried, I really did, but I can't get past this. I can't be what you want, what you deserve. So I tried to do my best by you."

"By fucking killing yourself? What kind of moron are you?" Denny yelled incredulously.

"I did my best by making you as safe and secure as I could," Richard yelled back.

"I don't want safe and secure. I want someone to love me."

"You're gorgeous, you'll find someone else. I can't live with this."

"So you'll give up on me that easily? You won't fight for me?" Contempt and derision mixed with Denny's anger. "And you let me think we were worth fighting for. Whatever happened to Mr Do the Right Thing? I guess it doesn't count when it's me."

"Not won't. Can't." Richard reared up onto his knees, face gaining back some of its color with his temper as he pushed toward Denny. "I can't do this. I tried, I really did. But I can't live with it, with any of it. There's too much. The guilt for a start."

"You lived, he died. A lot of people have been through the same thing. Get over yourself and deal with it." They were nose-to-nose shouting now.

"Like that? The way he died?"

"If you're too fucking pigheaded to see that you're not guilty for that, then spread it around. The guy who sold you out is the guilty one. Him and the police."

Richard snorted in derision.

"And Stella, she was closer, she should have gone back. Harley could have, should have, and all the others. Detlef should have been there. Hell, he's such a genius, he should have known it was going down and got you all out beforehand. Spread the guilt. We're all guilty for allowing something like that to be possible. You don't get to keep it all for yourself."

"But it's not just the guilt. I can't stand his constant screaming in my head. It's driving me insane." Richard pulled at his hair as if it were somehow attached to the pain inside.

"So we'll turn the fucking radio up." Denny spat the words out.

"Yeah? It's all going to be as easy as that?" Richard could do derision as well. "What about the pictures that play in my mind? They're not just when I'm asleep. They hit anytime, when I'm not expecting them. One second I'm pruning plants, the next there's nothing but blood and guts. Grady's blood, Grady's guts. How're you going to stop those?" He was every bit as angry now.

"We'll find a way. We'll see the head doctors, do cognitive-visual-whatever therapy. Yes, I can use the computer and if I can find out stuff like that, the head shrink will have a whole heap of other ideas." Denny sucked in a huge breath, before letting it out slowly. "You don't get to just give up on me. We're worth more than that. You talk to me and together we find a way to deal with it all."

"We are worth more but—"

"No. No buts. I'm not having them. Not about us."

Richard sat back on his heels, face tipped up toward Denny. "But it's so much more than us or even him. It's like I was broken after he died and now I'm slowly coming apart. I don't know who to be any longer," he said simply.

Denny looked at him for a long moment. "Be yourself. There's no pressure for anything else, except of your own making," he said, quieter now. "Don't be so hard on yourself. You don't even have to ask for help, just take what's being shoved down your throat."

"But..." Richard licked at his parched lips, all the pain and confusion swimming across his face. Denny knew this was it, whatever he said now was the thing that was breaking Richard. "I don't know who I am," Richard admitted, his anger draining along with Denny's. "I don't feel like Grady Porter's Richard anymore. I can't be. My whole life's been wrapped up with him, it's who I am. But if I'm not that, then what?"

"You're you. You're Richard Bailey. You've earned enough respect and value on your own. You don't need to be anything else." Denny was just starting to understand. Richard was honorable, honest, and a hero all in his own right, but he didn't always see it and he certainly didn't feel it.

"That's okay for the world outside." Richard lifted a hand vaguely toward the window. "But you know how I am. I'm not really like how I seem on the outside, I'm...I feel lost and...I don't know who I am."

"You're mine," Denny said. He might not have completely understood Richard's insecurities but he knew what to do about this, and it came completely naturally. Richard was his, and he was going to take what was his and keep it. "You're mine, that's who you are."

He reached out to hold Richard's face, hands firm, stroking his fingers, possessive. "I'm not going to let you go soft and take the easy way. You're going to fight and fuck up and fight again because we deserve that." He had to make Richard know, make him understand, and there was only one way to do it, with the goddamned fucking truth.

"I'm taking control now and I'm telling you, you're going to fight and I'm going to make you." He pressed Richard's face a little tighter. "Because now and forever, you're Denny Webster's Richard."

"Yours?" Richard's voice was breathy, almost needy. Denny had never heard it like that before.

Richard was finally giving up the last of that steely control.

Giving it to Denny.

"Yeah, mine." And Denny had never felt surer about anything in his life. Him, the ex-slave that had been bought and sold like a piece of cheap meat, fucked and fucked over until he didn't know how to think. Well, if Richard wasn't exactly what he appeared on the outside, neither was he. "Will that do you?"

"It's a hell of a start." Richard looked up at him as though his whole life depended on keeping that connection. "Hang on to me." He said the words with more vulnerability than Denny thought possible.

"I will." Denny cupped his fingers tighter around Richard's face. "I'll hold onto you while you mend, because you're mine now and I'm not losing you or letting you forget it."

Then all of a sudden Denny pushed Richard back onto the bed with a firm hand against his chest and flipped him skillfully onto his belly so he landed with a whump. "I think right now, we need to start with this, just so you'll know." He pulled the sides of the gray hospital gown apart, exposing Richard's naked backside. Running a hand down his spine, he dipped into the cleft.

"Now? Here?" Richard looked back over his shoulder.

"You got a problem with that?" Denny asked.

Richard seemed to think, but only for a nanosecond. "Not a one."

"Good." Denny stretched over him, already unzipping his jeans. "What can we use for lube?"

"You'll think of something, I have faith in you." Richard closed his eyes, sighing, and Denny could feel the tension in his muscles releasing along with the breath.

Denny slipped in a greasy finger and Richard sighed again. "Maybe I can make it because…because you'll stop me from going crazy or floating away." Richard spread his legs obscenely wide as Denny pressed his cock into him.

"Use me as an anchor," Denny said.

Richard wasn't quite ready and it wasn't quite slick enough but it was just about perfect. And just what they both needed.

"Mine," Denny whispered into his ear, and Richard managed to smile against the pillow.

Chapter Ten

"Hiya," Denny said while he peeled another potato and popped it in the pan of water. It landed with a splash just as Richard came in the door. "How did it go?"

"Okay." Richard put his keys on the side table and dumped his jacket on the chair. "More of the same. That woman is relentless."

"Pam's also supposed to be the best head doctor around. I made Detlef check about a million times."

"You know she hates being called a 'head doctor'." Richard got out two bottles of beer then handed one to Denny.

"I know. That's why I do it." Denny grinned. "It's my own petty way of getting back at her for pushing, although I know that's really a good thing. Apparently pettiness is my coping strategy."

"You're sad. I hope you know that." Richard leaned back against the counter and watched Denny work.

"But it really went okay?" Denny asked.

"Yeah."

"And nothing...?"

"No. I started thinking about something, though. Nothing to do with her. We were talking about one thing and then I thought of something else and, you know how it is." Richard folded his arms over his chest. "I stopped in the park on the way back. Didn't get out of the car, just sat and looked at the trees through the windshield."

"I noticed you were late," Denny said softly. "But do you see me not worrying? I'm getting good, aren't I?"

"I should have called."

"No, you shouldn't have." Denny lit the gas under the potatoes, his gaze going briefly to Richard. "You're doing better and you need your space. What is it she says? You have to be honest with me and tell me how you're feeling, and I have to trust you and give you the room to handle things. Something like that."

"Exactly like that. Except she uses longer words and more of them." Richard smiled.

Richard had been seeing the psychiatrist since before he got out of the hospital, sometimes on his own, sometimes with Denny. She was helping more than either had expected. She listened, prodded when needed, stood firm when necessary. She took no prisoners, making them both face things they didn't want to. But most importantly, she gave sensible, practical advice on how to cope, something Richard said he could have hugged her for, if he could have got his arms around her. She was a big, smiling, capable woman. Denny knew the last thing Richard wanted was someone trying to get him to talk about his feelings all the time. He needed concrete strategies for dealing with a concrete problem. Dr Pam Kaufmann had proven to be the woman for the job.

Richard had started off seeing her every day. Now they were down to two or three times a week or whenever he needed her. He'd sheepishly admitted to Denny that it was still more often than he would have liked, but he got along with her down-to-earth style and almost grandmotherly way of talking. Denny knew she'd been good for him and he'd even made Richard see that. The scars inside were healing along with the ones on the outside. But just as the long, jagged lines up Richard's wrists would never fade completely, neither would the wounds inside him.

"Do you want to tell me what you were thinking about?" Denny asked. "There's no pressure, honest. It's your call."

Richard pushed away from the counter. "Wait here. There's something I want to show you." He disappeared into the bedroom and Denny could hear the sounds of him rooting around in the back of the chest of drawers. A few minutes later he was back, a small, worn-looking brown envelope in his hand. "Come and sit." He pulled out a couple of chairs at the table before dropping into one.

Denny wiped his hands, turned off the gas on the stove, then sat next to him. "What is it?"

Richard huffed out a small breath, bit at his bottom lip, then took out a photograph then handed it over. It was torn around the edges with a thick crease along the bottom, but it was still clear. "That's Grady and me, years and years ago, when he'd only been free a year or so."

"How old were you?" Denny had to ask.

The photo showed Grady sitting crossed-legged in a field of long grass, his hair blowing across his face. His smile was about a mile wide and his eyes sparkled. Richard was kneeling behind, arms wrapped tight around him, appearing as though he were about to topple over into Grady's lap. His face was full of laughter, his smile every bit as wide.

"I was about nineteen, maybe twenty. He'd have been about twenty-two or three."

"My God. I never realized you were so pretty when you were young." Denny had to laugh. "Detlef said you were but I didn't think he meant that pretty. Both of you."

"Grady was gorgeous, and when he smiled..." Richard leaned in toward Denny and the picture.

"Plus skinny. You haven't got half the muscle you have now."

"I thought I was such a man back then." Richard smiled, but it was small and subtle. "Only I look more like a girl."

"It's the hair. Look at you with floppy hair. I mean, I know it's you, you're still recognizable, but you look so different. Grady as well. He could have almost put his hair in pigtails."

"He used to do this thing all the time, it always made me laugh." Richard reached out to stroke across the picture, not attempting to take it from Denny's hand. "He used to blow upward to try and get his hair out of his eyes, and it would puff out at the front. He'd look really stupid but he'd always check to see if I was watching and then grin. It was like it was our thing, just for me, and he carried on doing it long after he got his hair cut."

"That's soppy." Denny smiled as well. "Soppy and sweet."

"We were sweet back then. Sweet as you could be after all he'd been through. I guess we were kind of high on being away from my father and the start of the freedom movement. Those were good times, good memories."

"And you shouldn't forget them, shouldn't let what's happened supersede them." Denny rested his thumb rest on Richard's wrist, tracing along the small part of the scar showing above his cuff.

"I'm trying really hard not to, but..." Richard licked at his lips, the smile gone. "Pam said the same sort of thing today and it got me thinking about the photo. I was telling her how I could be thinking about something good, something positive, and all of a sudden an image or a sound will come into my head and all the good's gone. In a split second everything flips and the world seems black. She was saying that I have to let it flip the other way as well, bad to good. I can't let the bad bleed over into the good if I don't allow the reverse."

Denny thought about it for a long moment. "That makes sense. She's right. You can't let the bad be stronger than the good."

"That's what I'm trying to do. It isn't all that easy, but..."

"And you can't feel guilty when it does happen, when you flip from good to bad. I know you—you'll feel like you're letting that Grady down." He tapped the photograph with a finger. "If you let the world around you turn bad when you're thinking about that version of him."

Richard stared at Denny, his face serious. "How the fuck, out of all the people it could have been, did I get lucky enough to buy your freedom?"

"Huh?"

"How'd I get so lucky? I knew there were a million and a half reasons why I love you but this has to be a major one. Jesus fuck, Grady would have been fascinated by you, and he'd be so pleased for me, and…" Richard ground to a halt and sat, shaking his head, simply gazing at Denny.

"What I'd do?" Denny asked.

"How many guys would actually be interested in pictures of an old lover? Would let me talk about him for hours at a time?"

"Grady's important to you. I—"

Richard cut him off. "How many would know me so well they could work out what I was doing before I did?"

"Now I have no idea what you're talking about." Denny grinned, wrinkling his nose up in confusion.

"I didn't talk about this with Pam. Didn't work it out myself until I sat staring at the trees. But you knew. You said I feel guilty for letting Grady down because I can't prevent the bad flipping in, and I do. That's exactly what I do, but I shouldn't."

"Keep talking. I'm with you so far, I think," Denny said.

"This picture, how do we both seem in it?"

Denny studied it again. Richard with his arms possessive and loving around Grady, Grady holding onto Richard's hands, his whole face lit up and shining with 'mine'. "Happy. You look truly happy."

"We were, we really were. We'd set the camera up on a rock. Had about ten tries at getting it to go off automatically and were laughing ourselves stupid by the time we managed it. Right after that picture was taken Grady pulled me over and I ended up in the grass with him on top of me. Next thing we were kissing and touching and, you know how it goes. One minute I had my hand up his shirt, the next I'm naked on my belly and he's fucking me." Richard stopped, staring intently at the photo. "It was good, as good as it got for us. The feel of him inside me was just amazing. I made some kind of noise and then it all flipped. He flipped."

Again Richard stroked over the picture, his finger as gentle as possible.

"What happened?"

"I remember rolling over, the grass prickly against my back, and he was standing over me. His face was as white as a ghost's, the skin all stretched tight. He'd caught the sun in the days before, he had a bit of a tan, even burned his nose a little and it looked weird with his face so white underneath it. All he had on was his open shirt and his socks. His cock was still slick from me. It should have been funny but it wasn't. He was screaming and shouting about how he'd hurt me, how he knew that sound, knew it meant I was hurting. About how I couldn't do that to him. That I couldn't let him hurt me, let him become one of them. One of those people who got their kicks by hurting pretty young boys."

Richard glanced up, his eyes open and honest. "He didn't hurt me, not really. It wasn't like it is with you but I wasn't in serious pain and I wanted him. You understand, don't you? You believe me?"

"Yeah, I get it." Denny nodded. "Sometimes a bit of discomfort is worth it for what you're getting."

"Exactly," Richard said. "But what did hurt was when he walked away from me. It didn't last long and he didn't go far, but that hurt like all fuck. He came back and we talked and kissed, but for a few hours it wasn't the same. There was a strain around us. We went to sleep that night wrapped up in each other and we were back to normal the next morning but...that hurt."

Richard stroked once more over the photograph, then along Denny's arm until he rested his hand in the crook of Denny's elbow.

"You're right. I shouldn't feel guilty for letting the dark sneak in. I can't help it and neither could Grady. I'd kind of deliberately forgotten that, but he couldn't stop it, not even the amazing Grady Porter who could do anything. What I have to fight is letting it stay. I owe it to you, to me, and in a way, to him. He'd be mad as hell at me if he thought he'd been the cause of my unhappiness, and if he could, he'd sure kick my ass for it."

"Well, as he can't, I guess that makes it my job to kick your ass," Denny said. "Just remember I'm doing it for him. But..." He stopped for a moment, making sure Richard was watching him. "You don't get kicked for letting the dark in or even for letting it stay. You only get kicked for not trying to get rid of it. Even then we can only expect so much."

"See, you understand again. It's about trying, not about getting it right." Richard smiled, little licks curling at his lips, warming his eyes. "That's why I got so lucky with you."

"Nearly as lucky as I did," Denny said softly, but it was goddamned heartfelt.

Richard watched him for a moment, lip caught between his teeth. Then he ducked his head. It was an insignificant gesture but Denny saw it, knew it meant Richard wasn't sure about what he was going to say next.

"How come?" He hesitated before going on. "How come you don't mind me talking about Grady?"

Denny shrugged, not having to stop and think about it. "Because I know how much you love him, how much a part of you he is."

"That's a good thing?"

"Yeah. Because if you love him like that then maybe, just maybe, you'll love me the same way."

Richard flushed, the color flowing over his face in a wave that was so noticeable it was downright funny. His eyes shifted, going just about everywhere before finding their way back to Denny's face, almost shyly.

"I do," he said in a tiny voice, before clearing his throat and trying it again. "I do love you. Every bit as much as I love him. But it's different. Not less, just different. In a good way. Good different. You're different, so it's different, but good and—"

"Stop." Denny pressed his hand down on Richard's, smiling warmly. "I get it. I know what you mean."

"But you should know," Richard went on, determined. "You're not less than him or second, you're..." Richard seemed to fight to find the right way to say it. "You're after. I loved him first because I knew him first, and then you after. It's not less, just in sequence."

"That's what I'd hoped." Now Denny was finding it hard to say the words. "You love completely, with everything you've got, and I want that. I've never had anything like it before. Never really had anyone love me and then you came along and the way you love and... I want you to love me like you love him."

"I do," Richard said simply.

"It doesn't get any better than that."

"You know that you're the only reason I'm still here, don't you?" Richard scrunched up his face. "It's hard saying this stuff, but you should know. I don't mean I'm still here because you found me, but because I'd have done it again. I would have made sure I did it properly if it wasn't for you. Dying is the easy way. When you told me to make a decision to change how I was acting after the DVD, dying was the easy option. The only reason I fight now is you."

"Have you any idea how that makes me feel? I've never been important to anyone and—" Denny pressed a hand against his mouth, thoughts and feelings clouding his mind, making it hard to think. Hard to say things right. "I love you so fucking much and it's got nothing to do with what you've given me, all the chances, the way you push and make me think. When I saw you on the bathroom floor covered in blood and I thought you were going to die, it was you I loved, wanted. Nothing else, just you. Yeah, sometimes I get jealous of Grady because he got you first, but you're mine now and I'm not letting go."

"I get jealous too," Richard admitted. "I hate the thought of you with anyone else. I know you had no choice and there were a fair few, but I hate it in a way I never thought I'd feel." He raised his arms, staring at his hands balled tightly into fists. "I want to hurt anyone who ever touched you."

"Don't bother." Denny put his hands over Richard's again. "No one else mattered."

"But how do I stop myself from being jealous?"

"By knowing I've never loved anyone but you."

Richard looked at him, eyes wide and sincere. "So how do you stop yourself feeling the same way?"

"By knowing you've never fucked anyone but me and you're never going to." Denny smiled confidently. "See? Sex does have some uses."

"I..." Richard grinned, shaking his head. "I love you."

"Of course you do, because I'm adorable." Denny grinned back. "Now do you have any more photos for me to see? Come on, I deserve to laugh at your hair."

Richard smiled with him, and Denny could see him relax just a little more. "Only a couple. Most everything got lost along the way. These were only saved because I had them on me all the time."

"So go get the others." Denny pushed at Richard's arm gently. "At least I know that although you might have been young and pretty, I was even younger."

"And prettier, I'll bet," Richard said as he went to find the other photographs.

Denny just sat back in his chair and watched. So Richard thought he'd gotten lucky. Denny might be younger, and maybe even prettier, but he was damned certain he was luckier.

He was also quietly confident that with Pam's help, they were going to make it.

* * * *

Good days and bad days.

Richard thought about that as he busted his back digging a huge trench at the top of their land. He had good days and bad days, but it was the ratio that was important. The numbers were getting better, working more in his favor. Yeah, the bad days could be shit. Real honest-to-God shit that made him feel like he was drowning in the stuff but... He thought about that as well.

Were they as bad?

Some were, no doubt about it. Some days were downright fucking awful... But maybe they didn't always last the entire day, leaving him feeling exhausted and hating the world, like they had at the start. Perhaps the bad times actually were getting shorter, less frequent and not as intense.

Still hurt like a bitch, though. Still made him feel guilty as hell and... Focus on the good, not the bad.

Sweet Jesus, he not only had a psychiatrist but he listened to her and actually acted on what she said. Grady would have laughed his ass off at that.

No, Grady would have understood.

Denny would have made him.

That thought made Richard smile, the thought of Denny and Grady arguing over what was right for him. He could just imagine the pair of them, Denny with his miles of hard muscle, Grady with his pretty face and willpower of steel that you crossed at your peril. They'd have fought like a couple of alley cats and loved each other dearly afterward.

He really was a lucky bastard.

He hitched his spade over his shoulder and trudged back to the house, the grin still curling at his lips.

Yep, good days and bad days.

Denny was sitting at the table when Richard got in, working through a pile of receipts, looking bored to tears with the job. "Did you finish the ditch?" he asked, head still bent over his task. "We need to get the new drainage in if anything is to grow properly up there."

"Yes. Although I still don't see why I had to do it." Richard left his boots by the back door and went over to the sink to wash the mud off his hands.

"I'd rather have done that than go through all of this but, oh—" Denny stopped, looking at Richard, a dark grin slip-sliding across his face. "Come here."

"Why? Are you stuck again?" Richard dropped the towel and moved next to Denny.

"No." Without any attempt at subtlety, Denny caught hold of him by the belt, twisting on the chair so he could pull Richard between his spread thighs. "You're doing all right, yeah?"

"Yeah."

"A good day?"

"Yeah. Why?"

"Because..." Denny flicked Richard's buckle open then pushed his jeans off the curve of his hips. "You're all sweaty and you know how that makes me want to suck your dick."

"Now?" Richard wasn't going to squeak, he fucking wasn't. Even if his cock had suddenly got very interested in the idea. Traitorous son of a bitch.

"Right now." Denny slid Richard's jeans and boxers down and off.

"Bedroom?" Richard asked as Denny's hands fixed on his hips.

"Not a chance." Denny pushed until Richard was perched on the edge of the table, feet just about on the floor. "I want it like this. You all vulnerable and exposed, me all possessive and in control."

"You kinky bastard," Richard said, but went willingly enough when Denny put a hand on his chest and shoved. He lay back across the table and the receipts, not caring how he crumpled them, lifting his hands up to rub across his eyes. "You have to scrub the table after, though. That's definitely your job."

"Shut up and enjoy." Denny spread Richard's legs with the sheer width of his shoulders between them, leaning in to run his open mouth up the length of Richard's cock. He inhaled nosily. "Fuck, I really do like your sweat. It's all man and—" He lapped at the head, rolling his tongue into the slit. "I love your cock, it's gorgeous."

"Cocks can't be gorgeous, they're just cocks."

Denny sucked at the tip, a quick teaser, then slicked his lips before slipping them on and off with a wet pop of sound. "Yours is. Yours is the most beautiful cock I've ever seen."

"You make a habit of looking at other guy's cocks?"

"Doesn't cost anything to look." Denny tightened the ring of his lips and made a few passing swipes up and down. "I've seen a fair few, in the shower and other places. Yours is just the right thickness for me, just the right length."

"I'm surprised you didn't get arrested or beaten up." Richard let out a long, slow breath and relaxed back onto the table. One foot didn't quite reach the floor anymore, so he hooked it up on the chair behind Denny. Now he really was open and vulnerable, laid out on a plate for Denny.

"I let them look at mine in return and I could charge for that." Denny sucked at the tip again, his lips popping on and off before he suddenly took the whole thing deep for a moment. "Fuck, I love the feel of you filling my mouth."

Richard made a small groaning noise, almost sounding like he was in pain. "Arrogant bastard," he managed to say, although even he could hear the rise in his voice. He kind of knew he'd already called Denny a bastard once but hell, how was a guy meant to concentrate in circumstances like these?

"You saying my cock's not good enough to warrant a fee?" Denny sucked again, hard, but not with the rhythm Richard liked. It still managed to trigger another moan, though. Denny ran a hand up Richard's thigh, pressing a thumb into his groin, spreading his palm out flat to cover as much flesh as he could. Then Denny hollowed his cheeks and flexed his tongue against the underside.

"I'd probably pay to see it," Richard admitted, panting as he fought to pull enough air into his lungs. "I think your cock's pretty magnificent and that's before you do anything with it. But then, I am kind of biased."

"Yours is better." Denny cupped Richard's balls, timing each squeeze with his licks and sucks. Richard had no choice but to arch up off the table. "Yours would win first prize in the world beauty pageant for cocks." He pressed down, taking in as much as possible, sucking hard when he pulled back up.

"You're a fucking idiot. That's..." Richard scrabbled across the table trying to find something, anything, to hang on to as his chest heaved and his hips thrust up. He reached forward and dug a hand into Denny's hair, holding him in place while he thrust his cock in deeper. Richard couldn't help it, couldn't stop himself if he tried, and it was all Denny's fault for finding this uncontrolled response and dragging it out of him.

Denny gave a grunt of approval and kept sucking.

Pushing down against the table, Richard scrubbed his free hand over his face, trying to keep in the desperate noises while he hid behind his palm. With another of Denny's precise sucks and a squeeze to his balls, he gave up, throwing his head back as the skin on his neck stretched tightly across his Adam's apple.

Denny rubbed his hand across Richard's belly, pushing his shirt up and out the way before dropping it to open his own jeans and palm at his cock, pulling it free of the fabric. He pressed his face in closer as Richard lifted a thigh, pushing it against Denny. "Fuck," Denny mumbled, momentarily coming up for air. "Sweat and man and...I want to bite. Want to show the whole fucking world just who gets to lay you out like this, so desperate and so mine. Want to show who can make you give yourself so completely."

"Please," Richard panted, voice breathy and small, his hand still firm in Denny's hair. "Please, please, please."

Denny did just what Richard needed, timing his hands—one on Richard's balls, the other on his own dick—while he sucked and bobbed. Richard's hips rolled, almost past thrusting now as they stuttered, his cock sliding slickly between Denny's lips.

A squeeze.

Another.

A constriction of Denny's throat that went beyond sucking. Holding longer, pressure stronger and…

Richard's belly shook and his body convulsed with little shudders. He grabbed at Denny's head as he thrust up and in. "Oh fucking fuck," Richard managed as every muscle tensed and his dick pulsed.

But still Denny didn't let him go, sucking and pushing in deeper while he worked himself furiously. Richard eased up gently, his cock oversensitive now that he'd come. Denny pulled off, pressing his face into Richard's inner thigh, biting at his skin as he too came. He huffed against Richard's groin, making mumbled little sounds of pleasure.

"Man, you're good at that," Richard said as he petted Denny's hair. "I might just have to—" He didn't get any further than that when a loud gasp came from the doorway.

"Richard. Oh, I, oh. Oh." Stella stood, hand over her mouth, a red flush high on her cheeks.

"Oh fuck," Richard said for a completely different reason than last time. He closed his eyes tightly. Stella. Of all people, it had to be Stella. He'd forgotten she was due and here he was half-naked and laid out like a banquet.

"Like what you see?" Denny said, and just from the tone of his voice Richard knew he was grinning. "I do."

"You know," Stella replied, and Richard could tell that she'd recovered and got way more interested than he thought was right. "I rather think I do as well."

Richard decided he was going to stay right where he was, eyes covered, cock not, for the rest of his life. And if he ever changed his mind? He was never going to look Stella in the face ever again.

She'd love that.

* * * *

Somehow, over time and much to Richard's bemusement, they had developed favorite places to sit and talk. Not even obvious places at that. Number one had to be squashed in side by side on the back step, often passing a bottle of beer between them. Working on the land or moving around each other in the kitchen while they prepared dinner were also good places, but not really sitting.

It turned out that Denny liked to sit and talk. He said he could concentrate better that way and Richard had no choice but to go along with him. Denny also liked to touch him, and not just brushing a thigh or a hand on his back. No, he liked real, God's-honest, full-bodied contact, which was sort of how their latest position had come about.

They were sitting on the warm ground after full day's work with Denny's back against the wall at the top of their property. Richard sat between his splayed thighs, leaning onto Denny's chest, gazing out across their land. Richard didn't mind the dirt grinding into his ass. At times it felt like he'd been dirty half his life and now it just seemed comfortable. Natural.

"We've done good, haven't we?" Richard said. "If everything on the east side grows well, we might actually make money."

"Yeah." Denny rested a hand on Richard's shoulder. "Hang on—didn't we make money on the last harvest? I thought I bought my truck with that."

"We made money. 'Course we did," Richard reassured him. "I'm just not sure it covered all we spent to get going. I never got around to doing the sums, I couldn't see the point."

"All that work for nothing?"

"Not nothing. The equipment will last for years and we had to buy that. Plus we learned a lot."

"Maybe." Denny didn't sound convinced.

The sun was just starting to dip. Soon it would reach the top of the high hedge on the far side and everything would be washed in a golden glow. Richard liked that effect. It seemed almost magical. His hand went to Denny's thigh without his thinking about it. They had done well. They'd brought a patch of barren land back to life. That had to make a man feel good.

The silence stretched, easy and peaceful, until Richard hitched against Denny, pushing in closer. "I sort of had a thought that maybe we could move," he said tentatively. "Perhaps get a bigger place with more land, over near the foothills. Maybe a ranch or farm or something. What do you think?"

"Why? Why do you want to move now?"

"Because…" Richard hitched again.

"That's not enough of an answer," Denny said softly. "You know it's the sort of thing I've always dreamed of but it has to be what you want as well."

"I wouldn't mind a change from here," Richard admitted. "This was just a place to sleep and then you came along and sort of made it into a home. But then there were bad memories added to it. Only there's still you and that's good but..." He took a deep breath. "I wouldn't mind starting again. Somewhere that's ours from the start, that we can pick and plan together. Only if you want to, of course."

"Yeah, I want to," Denny said. "I'd really like that."

"Good." Richard relaxed even farther back.

"And horses. Can we get horses?"

"If you want. You decide. We can start looking for a place not too far away so it's close enough that we can get back as often as we like. But somewhere we can breathe and just be us."

"Just be us." Denny ran a hand through Richard's hair, just settling the strands. "I like that idea."

It was then that Richard noticed the two figures silhouetted against the sun. He didn't bother moving as they walked over. Neither did Denny.

"You look comfy." Detlef grinned down at them, dust spreading over the toes of his old boots.

"We are." Richard smiled, shielding his eyes against the sun as he looked up. "Although you could have brought us something cold to drink."

"Lazy bastard." But Harley was grinning as well.

"Bad news?" Richard's grin faded. "I mean, if it takes both of you to bring it."

"I honestly don't know," Detlef admitted. He squatted down next to them as Harley plonked himself cross-legged in the dirt close to Richard's legs. "I could lead up to this with a ton of small talk and explanation but it's probably easiest if I just tell you and let you decide."

Denny and Richard waited expectantly.

With a brief glance at Harley, Detlef went on in a quiet, straightforward voice. "We've found Grady's body. We didn't want to tell you before we were sure but we are now. We've got all the tests back and it's definitely Grady. Although, he's been dead a long time, so there's not much..." He let the sentence hang, knowing they would understand.

Grady.

Grady's body.

Richard closed his eyes and let himself rest back against Denny, feeling the sun on his face.

How did he feel?

Grady's body meant a grave or at least a place to visit.

A place to go and talk to Grady.

A chance to say goodbye.

To say I love you, I miss you, I'm sorry.

A chance to introduce him to Denny, stupid as that might sound.

Denny's hand still in his hair, Denny's long, firm thighs on either side of his. He felt the tears that threatened but would stay unshed.

He opened his eyes to Detlef and Harley's concerned faces.

"I want a funeral. A real one." He twisted his neck around to look up at Denny. Denny nodded and smiled.

"I'm glad you said that." Harley gripped Richard's ankle. "It's what I want as well, what Grady deserves. He should be laid to rest properly."

"I hoped you'd feel that way," Detlef said. "It seems like the right thing to do."

For a few minutes they sat quietly staring into nothing, thinking their own thoughts, remembering their own memories.

Then Detlef's gaze focused, first on all of them, then narrowing to Richard. "It's up to you," he said slowly. "But we have to decide what kind of funeral to hold. Do you want something small, just those that were close to him, or do you want something bigger?"

"What do you mean, bigger?" Richard asked.

"I don't know. It could be the whole of the movement or maybe even bigger. A celebration of his life, something the whole country can get behind."

"Turn him into a national hero?" Richard questioned, testing out the idea.

"He's that already," Denny said. "I knew about Grady Porter, followed what he was doing the best I could, even up where I was. He and Detlef gave me hope."

"There's no pressure, Richard," Detlef went on. "This has to come as yet another shock, right when you don't need it, when you're doing better. Take your time, think about it. It's your decision if you want it. We'll help you out if you can't handle it."

"I'll handle it," Richard said, voice sure and steady. "This is the last thing I can do for him. I'm going to do it right."

"Okay." Detlef stood up. "I'll call you tomorrow just to see how you're doing. There's no rush. Like you said, this should be done right." He patted Richard's shoulder, doing the same to Denny, and then was gone.

"You have Stella to thank for that," Harley said as Detlef rounded the edge of the house and was lost from sight.

"What do you mean?" Richard asked.

"Detlef was already planning his own thing when Stella put her foot down and said no, that it was up to you. I wouldn't have let him take over, but she got in first." Harley sounded a little amazed by that.

"What did she say?" Denny sounded a bit shocked as well.

"That she wasn't having Detlef stealing Grady. That he belonged to Richard and therefore it was up to Richard—and only Richard—as to what happened. She actually used the word 'stealing'. She was like an old-fashioned school teacher and we all just stood there and looked at her with our mouths open like real idiots."

"I'd like to have seen that," Richard said.

"How're you doing?" Harley asked after a moment, twisting around to see Richard better. "You were just getting straight and this is another jolt."

"A jolt maybe, but..." Richard sat up, not pulling away from Denny, just putting himself level with Harley. "This feels like a positive thing. I want... I want Grady to be at peace and this feels like a start."

Harley looked out over the growing plants, the new life. "Like the boss said, take your time deciding. There's only one chance at this."

* * * *

The thick hard slide of Denny's cock, the stretch and burn. Just enough to let Richard know, to remind him that he was here and alive. A fullness that filled his mind, an ache that reached from the balls of his feet to the back of his throat. A warmth around him that made him glad to still be breathing.

Richard rolled his hips back, not to get more dick but for more contact. More skin on skin, more firm muscle and hard bone pressed against his. More warmth.

That had been an unexpected phenomenon in the weeks after the DVD. Not at first, not when fire and hell filled his mind. But after Denny had told him he couldn't go on hurting himself. Told him to make a decision. When he'd done just that, made the decision to stop the nightmare, that's when the coldness had crept in. It had become so all-pervasive that he'd never felt warm, no matter how hard he worked, how much he sweated, how close he pulled Denny. The cold was in his belly and his head, covering his body like a second layer of skin.

Now he craved the warmth Denny gave him. Not only when they had sex, but when they were simply pressed together in bed, comfy, easy and warm. But it was good like this, when Denny covered him, surrounded him, pressed him into the mattress with his body, hard chest against his back, mouth on his neck, fingers twisted tight with his, cock buried deep, deep, deep in his ass.

He exhaled slowly, squeezing his eyes shut tighter so he could simply enjoy all that this was.

Denny stroked down Richard's body, digging under him, as his dick kept up its relentless rhythm, gliding into him slowly and deeply. Denny curled his hand around Richard's cock and started to pull in counter-rhythm, but...

"No, don't." Richard pushed the hand away.

"Ritchie?" Denny asked, close to his ear.

"If you do that then I'll come and I don't want to. I want this to last as long as possible."

Denny huffed, his open mouth against Richard's shoulder, breath damp over the sheen of sweat. "You don't have to ration yourself." Denny thrust again and again. "We have tomorrow and the next day and the next and...for as long as we've got on this earth."

Richard tried to twist his head, although it was stupid in his position. But he wanted Denny's mouth on his. "I'll take all that but I also want now. You told me once that you'd make me know about your cock in my ass. Well do it, make me know."

"Make you know?" This time Denny's huff was more of a laugh. He pulled his hips back, pressing in slowly and unrelenting, just as Richard liked. He kept a hand on Richard's waist, holding them tight together, his teeth raking across the scars on his shoulder. "I'll make you know about it, all right." He fucked deeper, harder, more thoroughly, until Richard was spreading his legs farther than they were supposed to go and he was humping into the bed.

"I want..." Richard's voice had turned into breathy little gasps of sound. "I can think better when you're inside me, clearer. It's like I can see things straight."

"Think better? That wasn't what I was aiming for." Denny chuckled against his shoulder. "I was kind of going for turning your brain to mush. But hell, if that's what you want, I'm happy to go with it."

"You keep going for as long as you like. I've got a lot of thinking to do," Richard said, pushing his face into the pillow and exhaling hard.

Denny smiled happily and kept going.

E p i l o g u e

Grady's funeral was held on a Friday, high in the mountains where the movement had first started. Richard had decided that it should be open for all who wanted to attend. No invitations. Come if you want to, if it meant something to you.

Thousands did.

They came any way they could, but almost all of them made the last part of the journey on foot, up into a small ravine, surrounded along the edges by tall pine trees. Quickly the place filled up until people had to just find a spot wherever there was room. They sat on top of boulders, gathered in groups across the scrub ground, anywhere they could see the makeshift podium.

Ex-slaves came from many, many miles around, as did former members of the movement. Those who had been closely involved and those just on the fringes all mingled together. People who had known Grady personally stood alongside others who had simply been inspired by him.

Old acquaintances embraced as they reunited, strangers made new friends.

At Richard's insistence, the word had gone out that this was to be not only a funeral but also a celebration of what Grady, and the movement as a whole, had achieved.

After the solemn part of the proceedings, they were to turn their faces to the sun and start looking forward. A last party before heading into the future.

Richard walked along with everyone else, greeting people as he went, accepting all the embraces that were offered. He smiled until the muscles in his face ached. He was among friends. He was comfortable with these people. He felt at home in the midst of the crowd. These were his people. All the while he held Denny's hand tightly, keeping him close.

He was looking to the future along with everyone else.

Stella took to the stage, welcoming everyone, explaining what was to happen and talking about Grady, who he'd been, what he'd done, what he'd meant to her. It was thrown open then, all and sundry coming up to share their reminiscences and tell their stories of Grady. Everyone had their chance to say what they wanted, and even Richard was surprised by how much Grady had meant to people. He stood to the side of the podium as they spoke, not wanting to do so himself, but a constant presence. His pride in Grady was sharp in his throat, but he was content to keep his memories to himself. Denny was close by his side and Richard made sure everyone saw him.

They all knew how much he loved Grady. It was only right they knew how he felt about Denny as well.

Detlef finished things up by making a speech that had tears running down everyone's cheeks. He had to keep repeatedly pushing his glasses back up his nose as even he cried. In the end, he was crying too hard for his words to be heard and he couldn't light the funeral pyre. Harley pulled him to one side when the crowd fell silent and Richard took the taper from his hand, lighting the tinder under the simple wooden coffin.

Then Richard stood back and watched while one part of his life burned away, rising as smoke and blowing across the tops of the trees. All the while his hand was twisted tightly in the heavy cotton of Denny's jacket sleeve, holding on to his future.

It was dark when the fire took hold, the flames vivid and strangely liberating against the night sky, the crackling sound loud to the silent crowd. All eyes stayed focused on the coffin as the edges caught alight, watching until the wood underneath it collapsed and it disappeared from sight.

Richard pulled Denny with him as he went to the microphone. "The past and all the sacrifices made will never be forgotten," he said simply, his voice under tight control when he looked at Denny. "But it's time to move on. Remember who we are, what we are, and what we stand for. But now let's go forward and make a better world."

As the crowd cheered he stepped back, Harley taking his place. "But first we party!" Harley roared.

That's what they did all through the night, around numerous bonfires. They danced and sang, got drunk and celebrated all that had been before thinking about the next day.

Richard partied with them, Denny close at his side.

In the early light of dawn, when all the fires had died away, Richard, Denny, Harley, Detlef, Stella, and a few others gathered together to dig the ashes of the funeral pyre into the ground. There would be no memorial, no grave as such, but still a place to visit.

A place for Grady to finally rest.

Soon the grass would grow again and there'd be nothing to show that anything had ever taken place. But Richard would know, the world would know. The world would remember Grady Porter, and that was what Richard thought mattered.

Then, his shoulder pressed against Denny's, they walked back down the mountainside.

About the Author

When Faith was clearing out her attic many years ago, she found a book she'd written as a ten-year-old. On rereading it she realized that it was the love story of two boys. Over the years her fascination with the image of beautiful young men, coiled together as they fell head over heels in love, became a passion for her.

Since that first innocent book—written in purple sparkly pen—she has written many stories, set in varied worlds, but always with two men finding their way to happiness.

Still nothing much has changed because now she can be found in a daydream, wandering around the supermarket, or sitting in a meeting at work still dreaming up stories.

Faith Ashlin loves to hear from readers. You can find her contact information, website details and author profile page at http://www.totallybound.com.

Totally Bound Publishing

Made in the USA
Monee, IL
19 June 2022